Book 3: The Airport Murder Mystery Series

Landing on Death

Padraic Regan

Edited by **Paul Byrne**

Copyright © 2023 | Padraic Regan |
All Rights Reserved

For my parents

The Airport Murder Mystery Series

The series based on the senses

Book 1   Forgotten (2021)

Book 2   These Roads He Walked (2022)

Book 3   Landing on Death (2023)

Book 4   No Other Way to Die (2024)

Book 5   Cancelled (2024)

Table of Contents

Prologue 8

Chapter 1 9

Chapter 2 13

Chapter 3 17

Chapter 4 23

Chapter 5 28

Chapter 6 35

Chapter 7 45

Chapter 8 58

Chapter 9 67

Chapter 10 74

Chapter 11 82

Chapter 12 87

Chapter 13 99

Chapter 14 103

Chapter 15 111

Chapter 16 119

Chapter 17 124

Chapter 18 128

Chapter 19 132

Chapter 20 137

Chapter 21 141

Chapter 22 147

Chapter 23 155

Chapter 24 161

Chapter 25 167

Chapter 26 175

Chapter 27 181

Chapter 28 187

Chapter 29 194

Chapter 30 199

Chapter 31 209

Chapter 32 219

Chapter 33 231

Chapter 34 240

Chapter 35 242

Chapter 36 251

Chapter 37 258

Chapter 38 266

Chapter 39 271

Chapter 40 276

Chapter 41 281

Chapter 42 285

Chapter 43 292

Chapter 44 295

Epilogue 302

Prologue

The driver of the excavator was pleased with his morning's work. He stepped down from his cab and surveyed the fifty metres of clearance that he had been working on. At this rate, the new runway will be ready ahead of schedule he was thinking as he leaned against the muddied yellow wheel arch. It looked like a broken clay plate when he first noticed it, about four metres away. Hoping that he hadn't unearthed the ancient relics of some medieval settlement, which would delay his work and ruin his holiday plans, he approached it cautiously. The closer he got, the clearer the fragments became. This isn't a smashed plate and this isn't ancient he said to himself as he reached into his pocket for his mobile phone.

This is the remains of a dead body.

Chapter 1

Marvelling at the keen eyesight of the driver, Detective Inspector Garoid Hennessy walked over to the remains again. The ground was dry from the warm summer weather and his wellington boots sank into the freshly dug-up clay with each step.

'Were you in the cab when you saw it?' asked Hennessy sizing up the height of the excavator driver which he guessed as being close to his own hundred and eighty-four centimetres.

'No, leaning against the wheel arch'.

Members of the Garda Technical Bureau were removing equipment from their white van and deploying it to preserve what might be declared as a crime scene. Hennessy had been requested, because no one else was available he believed, to conduct an initial investigation of the scene.

The call from the driver to his supervisor resulted in an immediate response and when the supervisor saw the remains, he rang the airport Garda station. Sergeant Tim Coady from the airport station inspected the finding first and then called in the investigators. The Airport Police – managed by the airport authorities – was also in attendance, its Incident Command Unit parked nearby.

'And you dug this area up this morning?' probed Hennessy as he looked at the mangled bones, scraps of clothing and what seemed to be pieces of flesh in front of him. A bent skeletal arm was stretching up diagonally about ten centimetres from what appeared to be a crushed skull and torso. Only about the top third of the body was visible, the remainder, assuming there was a remainder thought Hennessy, was still covered in clay.

'Yeah, I dig it up, loader puts it on the truck, and away it goes' replied the driver.

'When dya' think I can get back to work?' continued the driver as Hennessy was bending down for a closer examination.

Hennessy's facial expression provided the answer.

'Good to see you back in the field Gar, I heard you were back' said Coady as he positioned a metal barrier about three metres away. It was Hennessy's first time away from his desk-bound duties in the Criminal Investigation Department since being shot by a Detective Garda the previous year.

'Thanks Tim, what do you think we've got here?'

'Beats me, is Lubenski on the way?' asked Coady referring to the Chief State Pathologist Oskar Lubenski.

'Him or whoever's on call, could be a few hours they tell me. How long have these guys been working here?' queried Hennessy looking at the construction staff gathering around the driver who made the discovery.

'That particular company, couldn't tell you, but construction on the runway started nearly five years ago, delayed at various stages by Covid-19 of course. It's going to be over three thousand metres long and we're about what, five hundred metres from the east end of it? Should be possible to find out from the airport authority who's been working on different parts of it at different times. If you ask me, from just looking out the station window, there's been digging going on in this part for a few years' replied Coady.

'Can I ask you to step back from there please?' requested a technician in white overalls of Hennessy and Coady.

'Sure' said Coady, 'are you in charge on the technical side?'

'I am until the pathologist gets here. My name's Aoife Campbell, Senior Technical Officer. We're preserving the site first of all, screening and covering it, then we'll take photographs. Once the pathologist gives the okay, we start the trace evidence examination; could be a long night'.

'I'm going to declare it a suspicious death and potential crime scene while we wait for the pathologist's view' announced Hennessy.

'There'll be pressure from the construction company of course – it's an Irish and Spanish combined group I understand – to get back on site quickly, time is money' commented Coady.

'Likelihood of that happening is just above an ant's belly' said Hennessy knocking clay off his wellies.

Chapter 2

It was almost 6 pm when the State Pathologist arrived at the scene. STO Campbell briefed him on the work that had been carried out so far and offered him any assistance required. She also informed him that a construction worker with a Mediterranean accent had approached her twice about resuming work.

Lubenski started his work by considering the scene. The bones he could see still had scraps of what looked like clothing and possibly flesh attached or close by. There was a lot of insect activity also so he was thinking a forensic entomologist would be needed to examine the types and stages of bugs. The degree of body decomposition couldn't be established properly here, he quickly concluded, as the excavator may have caused some or all of the visible damage to the bones. He decided not to disturb the clay around where the remainder of the body should be in case he stood on bones where they shouldn't be. Then again, he couldn't be sure there was only one set of remains at this location, it could be a burial site for more than one body.

The colour of the bones and existence of what he believed were tiny pieces of insect-infested flesh told him that this person died relatively recently but that could still be up to a year, depending on the circumstances. A forensic anthropologist would be needed, he decided, to analyse the skeletal biology. He gingerly stepped over some of the clay to get closer to what looked to be the crushed skull. The material that had looked like flesh now looked more like cartilage and if it contained DNA, he was considering it to be the most likely scientific method available to identify the remains, as he wasn't hopeful at this point about the other two methods, fingerprints and dental analysis.

Lubenski called Campbell over and asked her to extend the area that had been screened off, explaining that there may be more bodies or skeletons.

'Will do Doctor, so we could be looking at a mass grave?' asked Campbell.

'I wouldn't be that dramatic Campbell but we need to be thorough' replied Lubenski.

'So this one has reached the fourth stage huh?' queried Campbell as she gazed at the bones.

Lubenski looked up in surprise.

'So you're a budding pathologist Campbell?'

'I take an interest yes, helps with the job'.

'The other three stages of body composition being...?' posed Lubenski.

'Autolysis, bloating, and active decay' replied Campbell.

'Good for you, some suggest five stages, inserting fresh as the first. So – '.

An aircraft took off from the main runway and stopped the conversation.

'So then you know' continued Lubenski after the pause, 'that there is no specific timeline for skeletisation to happen?'

'No but I presume it depends on location, humidity, et cetera, et cetera, et cetera?' answered Campbell.

'Correct' said Lubenski standing up to stretch out his full 190 cm frame, 'and of course the earlier the stage, the easier to identify. I'm going to have to call in a few experts on this one'.

'Now that you've confirmed it's human Doctor, I need to get more people and equipment here: lights, ground-penetrating radar, cadaver dog, the works' said Campbell, sounding almost excited at the prospect.

'I think I can confirm more than that' announced Lubenski bending down again closer to the partial skull. 'You see that small hole, in the temple above the right eye socket?'

As Campbell delicately crept forward to look, Lubenski finished his point.

'I'm fairly sure that was made by a bullet'.

Chapter 3

Hennessy was briefing Sergeant Tim Coady in the Airport station when a detective that he had worked with previously walked in to start her shift.

'Well behold what the cat dragged in! Looking good Gar' said face mask-wearing Detective Garda Anna Jenkinson.

'Good to see you AJ' said a smiling Hennessy as he put on his own face mask, 'appreciate the goodwill messages you sent'.

'I heard you were back on desk duties; how are you doing?' asked AJ.

'Apart from contracting Covid a few months ago, I'm good thanks'.

'You're looking leaner, and as dapper as ever. What brings you to Crime Central?'

'They found some bones on the construction site for the new runway, DI Hennessy was dispatched to investigate' interjected Coady.

'Because Brophy had no one else to send' said Hennessy referring to Detective Superintendent Marie Brophy of the Garda National Bureau of Criminal Investigation.

'Did I hear she's retiring, might be an opening for you Garoid?' suggested Coady.

Before Hennessy could respond, an anxious looking elderly man came in to the station and looked over at the three officers. He approached the public desk and told the officer on duty that he had lost his passport and was flying out to Paris for his daughter's wedding in two hours time.

Sergeant Coady went over to assist while Hennessy and AJ moved to the side of the building and sat down at her desk. The walls were a dark grey paint, the furnishings minimalist and despondent-looking, and the floor a dirty white and brown patterned linoleum. The warm temperatures left not so much a damp smell as one of dampness blended with hand sanitizer. A wooden box of old toys - used to placate lost children – idled forlornly in one corner. A fan on the end of the public counter turned right, clicked and turned left, mimicking the new recruits' passing out parade on Graduation Day at the Garda College. The notice board had two large posters displayed, both relating to Covid-19 regulations. A ray of sunshine glimmered through half-closed blinds, spotlighting a shimmering display of dust particles.

It was the first time Hennessy had visited the station since getting shot outside it and he thought he spotted some fresh paint on one wall which he surmised might have been part of bullet mark renovations.

'I heard you were involved in another murder case AJ, and that you pretty much solved it on your own. That on top of the suitcase murder you helped me with. What the fuck are you still doing in this graveyard?'

AJ noticed Hennessy didn't quite have the same arrogant swagger that he was known for before he was shot. He was dressed as usual in a tailored suit and he looked leaner but his tall frame seemed a little less upright, his beard a little less trimmed and his ginger hair a little greyer.

'You tell me Gar, you know exactly how I ended up here, you were involved for fuck's sake!' snapped AJ in reply, ignoring for the moment his use of the term 'helped me with' to describe her involvement in the investigation of a murdered girl found in a bag on an airport conveyor belt. Had he forgotten her contribution she wondered.

Hennessy sighed and leaned back in his chair. AJ thought she spotted a slight twitch of pain in his upper body as he adjusted himself.

'That's all water under the bridge AJ, you've more than made up for any misdemeanours in that Limerick saga. You should be a DS again, working with organised crime on all these gang hits'.

'Misdemeanours? The fuck you talking about? You threw me under the bus 'cos I took action to save a child's life and you fuckin' bottled it!' shouted AJ, her green eyes flaring.

Sergeant Coady looked over from the public desk at his two colleagues sitting no more than five metres away, his facial expression telling them to calm them.

AJ gave Coady an apologetic nod. Hennessy straightened up in his seat to give AJ an equally robust response to her outburst but appeared to think better of it at the last minute. He looked down at his hands, his face bearing more frown lines than AJ remembered, his fingers interlocked as if in prayer. It wasn't just the arrogance that was lacking, AJ thought, it was also his confidence levels.

'That was a long time ago AJ' Hennessy eventually mumbled, 'maybe I could have handled it better, maybe I could have stuck up for you more....but I told you not to fire – '.

'Stuck up for me *more*?' AJ interrupted, this time keeping her voice down, 'you didn't stand up for me at all, you did the opposite, you fucking blamed me'.

Hennessy fumbled with his hands again, this time also repositioning his feet under the side of the desk.

'I tried to make it up to you in my report on the suitcase homicide AJ, I said you were instrumental in solving it'.

AJ continued to stare at him, her anger subsiding as she reflected on the fact that Hennessy was shot defending her in that case, that he has a wife and a teenage daughter, that they were both ambitious when they fell out over the shooting incident in

Limerick, and that she might have done the same to him at the time if their roles were reversed.

'Anybody want us to help look for a missing passport in Terminal 1?' asks Coady, deliberately using a bit of humour to break in to the heated conversation between his two colleagues.

AJ and Hennessy both looked up at him in surprise.

'It's okay, it was handed in to the Airport Police. He shall go to the ball...or, wedding in this case' continued Coady, his with apparently wasted on the other two officers.

AJ used the break in hostilities to adjust her face mask and tidy up her already pretty tidy desk.

'I'd better go on a patrol' she announced. 'Who knows what dastardly crimes are being committed in this Covid-plagued airport while we guardians of the peace sit around gossiping'.

Hennessy's mobile rang as he stood up. It was STO Campbell. Hennessy listened, thanked her and hung up.

'Could be that things are going to get a little busier around here. Seems the remains are human...and the skull has a bullet hole'.

Chapter 4

'It's a conjunctive fucking adverb!'

'What is?' asked a stunned Hennessy.

'That is' came the response.

'Sorry ma'am, I – ', stammered Hennessy before he was interrupted.

'A subordinating adverb if you'd prefer or a fucking adverbial fucking conjunction but it is not....Hennessy, I'm not talking to you...hold the line please' said a clearly perturbed Marie Brophy.

Hennessy breathed a giant sigh of relief that she wasn't talking to him as he held his phone close enough to hear someone get an earful from his boss.

After a short pause, Brophy came back on the line.

'Apologies DS Hennessy but that admonishment you overheard was directed at a member of my staff who shamelessly disparaged the English language by misusing the term 'that is' in an important report, and not for the first time I might add. It's an affront to veracious grammar in my opinion, wouldn't you agree DS Hennessy?'

'Absolutely ma'am, nothing worse'.

Hennessy knew Brophy's reputation for eloquent words and foul language but he also knew her bark was worse than her bite and she was supportive of her officers when the higher echelons of the organisation were involved. Although slight in stature with black hair and green eyes, she was a steely County Cavan woman and had proven her worth in the field before moving to her present role. His relationship with her had started out a little shaky but he had grown to respect her judgement and her professionalism. With over thirty years service behind her, Hennessy had heard the rumour of her impending retirement that Coady had referenced. She kept her private life to herself but Hennessy understood that she was recently divorced and that her main spare time activity was playing golf.

'In any event Garoid, please tell me those skeletal remains you were checking out at the airport were those of a dead animal?'

'I'm afraid not ma'am, Lubenski says they're human and reckons there's a bullet hole in the skull' replies Hennessy.

'Fuck! Shite! Bollox! Whatever happened to remains being non-human or at least human but from natural causes or an accident? Why does every fucking body found in this bastardin' depraved city lately have to be a fucking murdered one?' exclaimed Brophy.

Hennessy deliberately didn't respond. He was in two minds about what to say next: should he request to lead the investigation or should he tell her what he was doing on site and stay schtum on the investigation team. What if he asked to lead the team and she said no, he'd look a right gobshite. What if she said yes; was he ready for frontline duties yet? The counselling people had cleared him to return to duty and he was allowed to carry a firearm but he was still availing of the Peer Support Service and he hadn't forgotten the incident in the car park at Dublin Airport, in fact just outside the station where he was now standing, that got him shot. He was quite certain he would never forget it. His main thoughts in the back of the ambulance that night were about the shock his wife Miriam and daughter Anais would get when they heard. That was another reason he had a lot of respect for Brophy; she handled the initial phone call to Miriam very sensitively and made a point of calling around to his house a few days later to talk to her. She had also visited him in hospital several times, telling him on one occasion that she was only calling in to get a break from the office for an hour.

Hennessy knew that resources were highly stretched due to the amount of feuding drug gang activity, not just in Dublin but all over the country. While he was still deliberating on what to say next, the decision was taken out of his hands.

'You'll have to head it up Garoid, at least temporarily. I don't have anybody else available and you have experience under your belt. I can't even offer you much in the way of experienced detectives to work on it with you but if it turns out to be another gangland hit, we may be able to roll it in to one of our ongoing investigations. What do you think? I know you were hurt last time out but you've passed all your return to work protocols; how do you feel about taking it on?'

The shock from being asked coupled with the shock of hearing Brophy talk so much without including a curse word left Hennessy temporarily lost for words.

'If you're confident I can do the job ma'am, happy to take it on' he replied after a brief pause. 'Thank you. I'm still on-site so I'll take it from here and give you regular updates'.

'Thank fuck for that!' Brophy responded. 'You'll use the airport station as your base I presume and I'll see who's around to help you. There is a detective based there at the moment that you've worked before if memory serves?'

Brophy knew bloody well the history between himself and AJ he was thinking to himself before answering.

'A very good detective ma'am, that is, I'd be happy to have her on the team'.

'I am very fucking impressed Garoid!' enthused Brophy.

'With what ma'am, my willingness to take on the case?' asked a confused Hennessy.

'Fuck no, with your correct use of the conjunctive adverb'.

Chapter 5

AJ had hoped to catch Lubenski before he left the scene but when she parked the station patrol car and got out, he was nowhere to be seen. She was glad Coady had intervened in her discussion with Hennessy when he did and headed straight for the construction site when she left the station.

There was a lot of activity now between the Garda technical staff, uniformed officers, and airport police. The lighting that had been set up by the technical crew made the area look a little macabre against the darkening sky and the white-suited staff allowed in to the cordoned off area added to the sombre scene.

AJ didn't recognise any of the people behind the face masks but one of them - diminutive in stature, energetic in demeanour - approached her as she moved closer to the barriers.

'Hi, I'm the Senior Technical Officer on site, Aoife Campbell; are you working on the case?' asked an enthusiastic Campbell.

'Detective Garda Anna Jenkinson, based at the station here; has Lubenski left?' replied AJ, deliberately avoiding the question but noticing a lock of red hair sticking out of Campbell's face mask in front of her right ear.

'Yeah, about fifteen minutes ago. He gave me instructions before he went so I'm actioning them now as well as our normal protocols in these situations'.

'Do we now how long this section of ground was here or when it was last disturbed?' queried AJ as she looked closely around the location.

'That's not my area Detective Jenkinson but I did see DI Hennessy talking to one of the construction staff'.

'You can call me AJ Aoife; are you planning to remove the remains tonight, do you mind if I take a closer look?' asked AJ, conscious that Hennessy might be just a few minutes behind her if Brophy puts him in charge of the inquiry and he might react badly to her presence there.

'We're setting up the portable X-ray system now, which will take a few hours to cover all the ground. You can get closer so long as you suit up and don't touch anything' answered Campbell.

The digital portable X-ray system that Campbell was referring to was a relatively recent addition to the tools available for the Technical Bureau and staff were still going through the learning curve in respect of its deployment. Setting up the equipment was quite straightforward as Campbell saw it, but using the software to capture and interpret the images was tricky. The machine was on wheels and looked a little like an army bomb disposal remote-controlled robot.

This scene was an ideal opportunity for Campbell to gain more field experience she was thinking to herself as she and a colleague assembled the unit. Campbell was young, highly educated and ambitious but her annual performance reviews had twice pointed out the need for more experience in the field.

The X-ray machine looked very cumbersome and complicated to AJ as, suitably prepared in her white forensic outfit and blue plastic shoe covers, she commenced her examination of the cordoned off area. The warm evening was already making the suit quite uncomfortable and she had only just started moving around in it. The visible skeleton parts struck her as a jigsaw puzzle with no particular starting point. It was difficult to establish if the small collections of material that appeared to be entwined on some of the bones were clothing parts, flesh, dirt, or a combination of all three. Nor could she see any bullet-sized hole in the skull but she daren't get as close as Lubenski did as the forensic staff were keeping a close eye on her.

    Despite months of deliberating over whether she wanted to stay in the guards, and discussing same with her live-in partner Ray, when moments like these arose – the finding of murdered remains – her adrenalin levels increased considerably. It seemed Garda Headquarters would never forgive her for discharging her firearm during a car chase in Limerick years ago. Another career option, requesting a transfer from the airport station, could land her in a remote part of the country - a peripatetic occupation she recalled DS Brophy once describing the career of a Garda as during an awards ceremony speech - that mightn't suit her or Ray. She marvelled at how easily she found it now to consider Ray and his needs in her career complications. Ray was a mechanic in a local garage but he also had his own customers that were increasing in number and he was determined to own his own business at some stage, hopefully before he reached forty.

AJ repositioned herself to try to figure out where the rest of the bones from this poor individual were but struggled to see any clear shape or outline. Was the body cut up after it was slain and different parts dumped in different places or did the excavation process damage a perfectly complete and normal murdered dead body, she asked herself as she moved around the site. She would have loved to use a pencil or stick to move some clay in order to check for where additional bones should be located but that could compromise evidence and land her in more trouble. She could hear the X-ray machine making whirring noises now as if it was taking images and that should reveal where the rest of the skeleton was, assuming it was here at all. It could also help identify if there is more than one body dumped here she thought as she stepped back near one of the metal barriers and tried to work out how the wheels of the machine weren't moving potentially evidence-bearing soil. It's probably too much to expect that the murder weapon would be found she figured but then again, that has happened before. She was anxious to approach Campbell to ask if they were getting any useful information from the scanning process but all four of the technical staff that she could see looked very busy. In any event, there was a limit to how much information she could expect them to divulge to her at this stage, assuming they had gathered anything of value. It may well be the case that data collection and data interpretation were two very distinct activities, a point that had been made by some of the scientific people that provided detective training at the Garda College in Templemore. Her thoughts were interrupted by somebody calling her name from where the Garda vehicles were parked about twenty metres to her immediate left.

It was Hennessy.

How the feck could he possibly have known it was me in all this forensics gear she wondered to herself as she turned to face him.

'Figured I'd find you here AJ, in the centre of the action' said Hennessy.

'I just thought I might be able to help you know...might see something or hear something' replied AJ in an apologetic tone, still taken with Hennessy's keen sight.

'And did you?' asked Hennessy.

'Eh, no...well, not yet' answered a surprised AJ.

'Better look and listen harder so, you're on my investigation team' said Hennessy.

'I am? You picked me? With our background and after the argument we just had? I don't know what to say?' spluttered a disbelieving AJ.

'I didn't pick you, Brophy did'.

Chapter 6

'What doesn't kill you makes you longer'.

'You said that to Stretch?' asked AJ

'No, he said it when we arrested him yesterday, eight time this year so far'

Speaking through face masks, AJ and an Airport Police Officer walked through Terminal 1 departures discussing a well known shop-thief – nicknamed Stretch because of his diminutive stature - who bought ten Euro airline tickets in order to access the airport's airside retail area where he proceeded to fill his empty bag with cigarettes. He would then return through the Arrivals area without ever flying. If Immigration or Customs – who don't know whether he has travelled or not -stop him, he claims to feel too unwell to make the trip.

'He was wearing a baseball cap and sun glasses last time I arrested him, hardly a master of disguise' quipped AJ.

'No criminal mastermind' said the Airport Police Officer, 'but he aggregates dozens of charges for each Court appearance and then gets a six-months' suspended sentence or something. Not sure if he's ever done time'.

'Gotta love the justice system' said AJ.

There were a few hundred early morning passengers circulating around the check-in islands which was a big increase over recent months but the regulations regarding face masks and social distancing made them look more nervous than excited about their forthcoming trips. Staff at the check-in desks behaved with a certain wariness as they spoke to passengers and handled their booking forms, passports and baggage. Two cleaning staff were operating floor sweepers inside the two entrance doors and several cabin crew members were hurrying towards the departures gates. Anyone unfortunate enough to have to cough or sneeze loudly were looked on with disdain.

Expanding rays of sunshine were seeping in through the fourteen, steel-framed architectural bays that decorated the front of the building with temperatures warm enough for a lot of short-sleeved shirts and shorts to be worn.

AJ was delighted to be officially assigned to a homicide investigation, even more so because it seems Brophy had made the decision. Maybe this is a turning point AJ was thinking to herself, maybe the powers that be in Garda HQ were finally beginning to forgive her. Maybe her work – official and unofficial – on two previous murder inquiries had been noticed after all? Where did that leave her with Hennessy she was also wondering, did he object to her being picked for his team? Hardly, given that he wouldn't dare disagree with Brophy, especially now that he's trying to work his way back on to front-line duties. Or was that objective she asked herself; he didn't seem as confident, as ambitious, as arrogant; maybe he's lost a bit of his bluster? Maybe he's delighted to have her on-board, especially as it's an airport-based case, she considered? He seemed happy enough when she suggested doing what she was now doing. Either way, she had to grab this opportunity and do her best on the investigation team; she could judge Hennessy's view of her involvement better as they worked together on it, assuming they were going to work together on it.

Before they arrived at the Airport Police Control Centre for AJ to review CCTV of the construction site, two different passengers had stopped them looking for directions.

'It's amazing how sensitised passengers eyesight is when they're going through an airport' the Airport Police Officer commented after one such request. 'They're constantly scanning the place for information signage: check-in desks, departures piers, boarding gates, baggage belts...you name it. Even when they're following the signs and walking the right way, they still regularly stop staff for looking for directions, for re-assurance I suppose. It's something to do with increased adrenalin levels they were telling us during training; seems it applies to all the senses. There's a whole science behind it'.

'So cocking their ears when they hear announcements on the public address system: final boarding call for flight blah, blah, blah, that kind of thing?' queried AJ.

'Yeah, that kind of thing. Even regular travellers sitting at their boarding gate look up when they hear final boarding calls for other flights. Anyway, this is us' said the Airport Police Officer opening the Control Centre door for AJ.

'Appreciate it. I know we can access some CCTV footage over in the station but we're not the best technically to view it properly and our equipment is fairly old' said AJ.

'When is the new Garda Station opening, that will have all the latest technology I'm sure?' asked the officer.

'Next Summer is the latest I've heard. Yeah, all singing, all dancing they're telling us' answered AJ, hoping that she wouldn't still be based there when it opens, 'and fifty Gardaí stationed in it, up from twelve now'.

'If the passenger numbers go back up after the Covid pandemic, I suppose they'll need them' said the Officer, introducing AJ to the other staff in the office, setting her up in front of a monitor, and then demonstrating how the different camera positions and directions relevant to the building site could be loaded and controlled.

The Control Centre was windowless but very well lit and decorated. The walls were painted a light blue and the natural stone flooring was a shiny dark grey. It was about ten metres square with one wall entirely filled with screens and two seated Airport Police Officers monitoring same. Two telephones and an industrial-looking walkie-talkie sat in front of each officer; one phone was vanilla in hue and the second one red. The red phones had three direct lines: air traffic control duty manager; Garda Headquarters in the Phoenix Park, County Dublin; and Army Headquarters in the Curragh, County Kildare.

'You know the basic layout of the airfield Detective:' said the airport police officer, pulling up an image of the airport campus, 'main runway on the south side running east to west, new runway or north runway parallel on the north side. Parallel means you can use them both at the same time, one for taking off, one for landing. There's a shorter crosswinds runway as well but it's mainly used for smaller aircraft: executive jets, private flying, that kind of thing'.

'It's a big area' said AJ trying to take in the details.

'The entire campus is two and a half thousand acres so the airside is probably the guts of two thousand of that. The perimeter fence is over fifteen kilometres in length' outlined the officer.

'One of the airport's four airside access points for vehicles, adjacent to Hangar Six in the aircraft maintenance area, has been designated for use by North Runway construction traffic', the officer continued as he zoomed in on an image of it. 'In addition, an emergency access gate at the east end of the Forrest Little Road is opened occasionally and temporarily for very large construction equipment, such as earth-moving diggers or high volume convoys, such as concrete pours. For security and insurance reasons, all motor vehicles had to be escorted by airport vehicles, usually airport police units, or operated by airside-trained drivers'.

'How many cars and trucks and pieces of equipment or we talking about?' asked AJ, thinking in terms of how the dead body got to the place it was found.

'Hundreds' replied the officer. 'Broadly speaking, there are two types: permanent ones, for motor vehicles and large pieces of equipment based here, and temporary ones. The permanent ones must display an AVP, an airside vehicle pass, which we charge for. There are over three hundred AVPs in use at the moment. Regarding the temporary vehicles, which are almost all working on construction jobs, they can operate within a construction site perimeter if they have undertaken airside training, but when airport escorts are required, we charge fifty to a hundred Euro for each one'.

'It's all strictly controlled then?' probed AJ.

'It has to be. It's not like driving on the public roads' the officer replied, 'where you might hit a truck or a bus. Here, you could smash into an Airbus A380 or a Boeing 747 Jumbo. They come in at around half a billion Euro each, that's why we require astronomical levels of insurance cover. We've also got the new Air Traffic Control tower under construction at the moment as well so it's a particularly busy time on the airfield'.

Truth be told, AJ wasn't really sure what she was looking for. It was too early in the investigation to have any particular time period or piece of equipment in mind. Her main objective therefore was to familiarise herself with the location of the cameras and quality of their images. The task should be much clearer she was thinking, when the medical and forensic reports are available.

'Do you have many crashes or driving infringements?' queried AJ.

'Thankfully, no. We get a few cowboys who think they can bend the rules, sometimes there are cultural issues as we have a lot of non-national workers here, but we have the power to ban them from accessing the airfield and for a lot of them, that's their job gone'.

'That concentrates the mind all right. When you say cultural issues, what exactly does that mean?' probed AJ.

'Well, for example, you probably know the two main contractors on the North Runway project are Spanish and Irish – hence the joint venture company is called Spire - so you can get the odd language translation problem but as I say, nothing we can't handle' answered the officer.

'What about the big fight?'

AJ and the officer assisting her both turned around at the same time to look at the source of the comment: one of the two Airport Police Officers staffing the Control Centre was staring back at them.

AJ was first to speak.

'What, a fight on the runway site between Spanish and Irish construction workers?'

'No, between two Irish blokes'.

Chapter 7

Detective Inspector Garoid Hennessy was beginning to regret that he had arranged to meet the two of them together. The interview in the airport's Garda Station conference room had degenerated into an unruly statistics competition.

On one side of the hardwood table sat the North Runway Project Manager for Pelago SL, Javier De Leon, a tall, slim, Barcelona-born man in his late fifties with green eyes, greying black hair, thick dark eyebrows and a square face. Directly across from him was the North Runway Project Manager for Sugarloaf Builders Ltd., Dylan O'Leary, a heavyset man from Bray, County Wicklow in his mid thirties with brown eyes, fair hair, and a chiselled jawline. Both men were wearing yellow, hi-viz jackets, light blue overalls and mucky, steel toe boots.

The detective had requested the two men to remove their face masks when they arrived, assuring them that they were sufficiently socially-distanced to comply with the Station's Covid regulations.

Having explained the reason for the interview and making it clear that he could give no undertaking at this early point in the investigation as to when construction could resume, he asked them to explain clearly their roles and the details of the work taking place at the crime scene site.

'This is a three hundred and twenty million Euro project, there are financial penalties if we do not meet the schedule' exclaimed De Leon, completely ignoring Hennessy's questions.

'We have over two hundred staff waiting to get back to work' chipped in O'Leary, 'will you pay them for sitting around on their backsides, fuck you will?'

'There are sixty four specialist Spanish engineers here, all on overseas allowances, what will I tell my bosses? That you found some shitty dinosaur bones so we have to wait for ever?' said De Leon in an accent that Hennessy increasingly believed reflected an English education at some point.

'Engineers my arse, they're bricks and mortar men, like the rest of us' said O'Leary derisively to De Leon.

'This isn't just some shitty little road we're building here, it's over three kilometres long and seventy-five metres wide. It has to be precisely parallel with the South Runway; that means one thousand six hundred and ninety metres apart at every point. Including the taxiways it's three hundred and six thousand square metres of new build' said De Leon, ignoring O'Leary's insulting comment.

An aircraft with red and white colouring taxied past and the conversation had to pause for about forty seconds. Outside the sun was shining from an almost cloudless blue sky and temperatures were heading towards 18 degrees Celsius.

'The whole build site is four and a half kilometres long by half a kilometre wide, it's colossal' said O'Leary after the intermission. 'I have forty-two concrete deliveries lined up this week alone for a big pour, it's C40 strength, that's industrial rigid pavement grade, you're looking at one hundred and fifty Euro per cubic metre, it's not like they can re-direct it to some fucking brickie building a fucking garden wall somewhere'.

'It's called the runway project but it's much more than a runway, we're installing fourteen kilometres of boundary fencing. It's nearly three metres high and has to be non-climb and allow electromagnetic waves to pass through. It's not the shitty little fence at the front of your house' said De Leon.

'Is that why you need your 'special Spanish engineers'? My arse!' said O'Leary to De Leon.

'You shut your shitty big mouth!' shouted De Leon in quick response, no longer prepared to tolerate the insults hurled by his counterpart, and banging his fists on the table at the same time to demonstrate his seriousness.

Hennessy tried not to think about how disappointed his boss would be with the limited variety and high repetitiveness of curse words utilised by the two men. He would let them vent for a bit longer, he decided, provided they didn't start throwing punches.

'The job has loads of other bits to it: re-directing six kilometres of perimeter roads, laying nine kilometres of piping for surface water and land drainage, putting in twelve navigational aids, seven and a half kilometres of electrical cable, four sets of instrument landing systems, two thousand new runway and taxiway lights...the list goes on and on' said O'Leary, trying to re-focus the conversation and avoid De Leon's Dracula-like eyes glaring at him.

'Like you go on and shitty on' blurted out De Leon.

O'Leary made a provocative re-positioning move in his seat.

'All right, enough. I'll ask the questions and you'll answer. We'll do it here, politely and expeditiously, or I'll bring you separately to Santry Garda station and do it there?' said Hennessy in as authoritative a tone as he could muster.

Neither of the project managers responded, continuing to stare at each other.

'Okay, I'll take your silence as agreement' said Hennessy after a short pause, 'now, first question: describe your exact role. You first Mr. De Leon please?'

'Alphabetically, your surname is first' clarified Hennessy when O'Leary gave him an aggrieved look.

'I am Javier Jorge Hugo De Leon. I work for Pelago Sociedad Limitiada. It is a highly respected Spanish infrastructure –'

'Sorry Mr. De Leon' interrupted Hennessy, 'I don't need too much background on your company today. If you could just focus on what your role is on-site, on a day to day basis please?'

O'Leary couldn't, nor did he wish to, hide his smug look.

Over the next twenty minutes, both men proceeded to outline their job descriptions for the runway construction project. They combined office functions like ordering supplies, checking deliveries, updating target achievement files, and submitting daily progress reports to their superiors with frontline responsibilities such as staff supervision, work quality checks, and equipment availability and functionality. Although they had several supervisors reporting in to them, Hennessy could see that neither project manager was afraid to get dirty or operate expensive machines themselves when someone didn't show up or couldn't be found at the time required.

Hennessy took notes and wasn't surprised at how similar their functions were; in fact he was impressed with the way tasks were distributed and co-ordinated between the two project managers and their respective teams. When they used terms like project management software and critical path analysis, he tried not to show his eyes glazing over but it was clear that both men were very experienced and competent at what they were doing. The more he listened the more he doubted that the petty squabbling he had witnessed earlier was allowed to interfere with their number one priority: getting the task completed as efficiently and effectively as possible. As they spoke, he was also beginning to understand why the two organisations had formed a Spire Limited to submit a proposal to, and eventually win, the international tender process involved in awarding the contract. The Spanish firm appeared to have more expertise and experience in sophisticated electrical engineering equipment installations whilst the Irish company knew all about largescale builds with heavy machinery and a lot of concrete; they complemented each other. The two men seemed to take pride in their work but there was a steely determinedness about them, a ruthlessness even.

At one point, O'Leary talked enthusiastically about the Gold Award in the Considerate Constructor's Scheme that his company had already won on phase one of the project. It was a first in Ireland and involved over eight thousand construction sites in Ireland and the UK getting measured by independent monitors under five headings: safety, community, environment, workforce, and appearance.

Although neither man mentioned it, Hennessy suspected each of these professionals stood to receive big bonuses for bringing this contract in on time and on budget. If that was the case, he surmised, more than their reputations were at stake. But were the stakes high enough he wondered, to be connected to the skull with the bullet hole?

Having satisfied himself that he fully understood their roles, the detective moved the conversation on to the second, and more important, question he had posed at the outset: what exactly was happening at the site where the skeletal remains were discovered?

As O'Leary was responsible for most of the excavating and earth-moving operations, he took a deep breath before responding.

'That part of the site is on the east end of the new runway. We've completed the surface and drainage works there so we're putting in the base of the runway, to start building up the layers'.

Hennessy continued jotting down notes without looking up.

'We're putting in the granular subgrade at the moment' O'Leary continued, 'which involves a lot of diggers levelling the ground and a lot of tipper trucks depositing and removing material'.

'So can you tell if the ground where the body was found has always been there and is now being dug up for the first time, or if it is earth that was brought in on your trucks from outside the airport?' queried Hennessy.

'The short answer is no' replied O'Leary.

Hennessy looked up sharply.

'I'm not trying to be smart Detective' continued O'Leary quickly, 'I've spoken to the drivers and I've looked at our drawings and programme charts, and I've walked around your cordon studying the ground but I still can't be definitive. The problem is that the main construction works on this site started in 2019, that's two years ago. In fact you could go back to July 2016 when the Site Investigations Works happened to try to trace the amount of times digging took place around that stretch of ground'.

'Site investigations works?' probed Hennessy.

'Yeah, to test the substructure' exclaimed O'Leary. 'They drill boreholes and dig trial pits. You're talking about a whole team of geotechnical engineers and archaeologists, and a lot of machinery'.

'So there could have been different types of ground works going on in that specific location for the past five years?'

'Not continuously but at different stages of the overall project, yes' confirmed O'Leary.

Hennessy knew that the medical specialists like forensic entomologists could help to narrow down how long both the soil and the skeleton have been in that piece of earth for but he was still worried about the sheer volume of different firms and people had access to that location in recent years.

'So go back to the work you've been doing there recently, if you have to remove earth as you level the ground in one area, could that then be tipped onto the site we're talking about?' queried Hennessy.

'It could eventually but not immediately, if that makes sense?' replied O'Leary.

The perplexed expression on the detective's face answered him.

'So, like I say, we're building up layers. The reason for the layers is so that the impact of an aircraft landing is dispersed downwards rather than sideways, to avoid cracking'.

'I understand that part but surely planes don't land all the way down the runway?' asked Hennessy.

'Exactly Detective, the heavier ones – and they're the ones we're mainly interested in here, commercial aircraft can weigh up to three hundred tonnes coming out of the factory and then add passengers, baggage and cargo – land within the first four hundred metres of the runway, at either end' clarified O'Leary.

'So you have more layers at each end?'

'Not more layers but thicker ones and we start the base further down as well' responded O'Leary.

'So that might make a more suitable place to dispose of a body, less chance of it being dug up?' probed Hennessy.

'That's your area of expertise detective, not mine'.

'I hope you're not suggesting that any of my staff could possibly be involved in such an act?' cut in De Leon, who was feeling a bit left out of the discussion.

Hennessy didn't respond; he continued taking notes for over a minute before resuming his questioning.

'You said 'not immediately' when I asked about excess ground from one area being used to fill in another area, what does that mean exactly?' asked Hennessy.

'It means that we focus on one stretch at a time so if we dig out a tonne of soil that we don't need in one area, we don't immediately use it as fill somewhere else, that's not efficient project management' said O'Leary.

'Does that mean you have piles of soil temporarily left all over the place?' probed Hennessy thinking that the remains might have been sitting in a mound of earth before ending up where they were found, or even that the body had been dumped initially in one of those temporary mounds.

'Absolutely not,' replied O'Leary, 'appearance is one of the criteria in the Considerate Constructor's Scheme, we run a tidy site. Any material we don't need each day is moved to our fill dump'.

'Fill dump?' probed Hennessy.

'Yeah, it's a field we rented at the east end of the Forrest Little Road, about a kilometre from the site, all material leaving or entering the site transits though it' clarified O'Leary.

'Detective, when can we expect a decision on getting back to work?' interjected a frustrated De Leon.

'When we're satisfied that we have collected all relevant evidence from the site' responded Hennessy firmly as he put his pen and diary back into his jacket and standing up from the table.

'But my superiors will not tolerate this delay, every hour is costing –'

'My priority is investigating a murder' interrupted Hennessy before De Leon could finish his point.

And that just got a lot more complicated, thought Hennessy to himself as he left the room, now that we could have a second crime scene.

Chapter 8

'Pivoting I think they call it, that's the in phrase these days' said Chief State Pathologist Oskar Lubenski, a tall, thin, bespectacled man with a square face and greying hair. He was wearing a medical-looking jacket and dark green slacks.

'Double pivots you even hear football managers talking about' commented Senior Technical Officer Aoife Campbell hoping she didn't come across as being too smart or mouthy. She knew that this was another good opportunity to gain experience and that she wouldn't have got it if her two supervisors weren't both unavailable; one was on leave and one had contracted Covid-19. She wondered if this qualified as a Homicide Case Conference and if therefore she could include it in her next application for promotion. She promptly decided that it did and she would.

'Whatever it's called, I appreciate you coming out here at such short notice Oskar, I know you've got a lot on...and you' said Hennessy looking a little less appreciatively at Campbell, her shoulder length red hair now clearly on display in the absence of a face mask and forensic hood. Standing about one and a half metres tall she looked much more casual in a purple sweatshirt, dark blue jeans and hiking boots.

'So you're thinking this is a second crime scene Gar' said AJ, the final member of the four people standing in the middle of the fill dump that O'Leary had informed Hennessy about earlier.

'Potentially, yes' answered Hennessy looking around the large field. He had been told it was about six acres in size, which he equated to approximately six standard-sized football pitches. Surrounded by a barbed wire fence and with at least six CCTV cameras in plain sight, there were dozens of mounds of material spread throughout the site. Some had metal sheeting secured around them but most lay uncovered. Others had temporary barriers surrounding them. The colours of the mounds were also numerous in number and the strong sunshine made some of the material glisten and other bits twinkle. The scene resembled the opening sequence of a film set in a post-apocalyptic world that had been laid waste by aliens or a deadly virus. The only entrance to the field was directly off the Forrest Little Road and just inside the heavy metal gates sat two large, green portable buildings.

Hennessy could see an aircraft with an image of a palm tree coming in to land on the main runway as he surveyed the site but it was too far away for its engine noise to interrupt their conversation.

'Earlier, I met the project managers from the two firms that are jointly building the new runway. They told me about this place: it's called a fill dump and basically, all material entering and leaving the construction site comes through here. Seems it helps them control deliveries and makes the building area look tidier' explained Hennessy.

'So our body might have passed through here?' queried AJ.

'Or been murdered here' spat out Campbell before thinking that it might not be her place to make that observation.

'That's what I wanted to talk through and why I wanted to have the discussion here, but we need the dump supervisor, Griffin, to join us and he's on a phone call in that first hut so it gives us a few minutes for any updates. I know it's still preliminary stuff and too soon for written reports but I'm conscious that we need to move quickly, and we need to let construction on the site resume as soon as possible'.

What had first struck AJ as an unorthodox but maybe creative location to hold a meeting was now beginning to look like something else, she was thinking as she looked around. Whatever about bringing her here, hauling the medical and forensics people out to a field full of earth beside the airport when they would surely be better tasked at analysing the material already collected, could be seen as a sign of strain, if not desperation. Maybe this was too soon after his gunshot injuries for her boss to be put in charge of a murder investigation? Maybe he was still suffering from some form of post-traumatic stress disorder even though the professionals had cleared him to return to frontline duties? AJ knew from dealing with the force's psychological experts, after discharging a firearm, that anxiety is not an exact science. Interviews with them are stressful in their own right, even before they drag up the details of whatever event you experienced. Then there's the old chestnut of how you answer their questions: do you give them the absolute truth as you understand it, or do you tell them what you think they need to hear in order to clear you, or some combination of both? Do the mental health experts know when you're lying; can they weed out the mistruths from the facts? It seemed to AJ that adrenaline levels are running so high at the time of the incident under discussion that you may not be recalling precise details accurately even when that is your intention. The mental consequences therefore, could be hinged on misinterpretations. Hopefully, Brophy won't detect any hint of panic when he updates her on the case. AJ understood that all lead investigators are under pressure to make progress but Hennessy had just mentioned another potential source of nervousness: allowing construction to get going again on the runway; he must be getting it in the neck from the builders and the airport authority. That was now further complicated by the discussion they were about to commence; if the fill dump is deemed a crime scene and all materials have to pass through it, how can construction restart?

'We've analysed the scene using standard protocols Detective Hennessy' said Campbell, jumping the gun in terms of seniority. 'Firstly, we used chemical reagents – effective up to six years after blood deposition - to test for latent bloodstains as none were visible, not unsurprisingly given the state of the remains. I can confirm that we did find evidence of blood and we've sent samples for analysis. Hopefully, those samples are of sufficient quality to gather biological information and possibly even extract DNA. We are also attempting to determine the volume of blood deposits; as you know, high volumes as you know equate to a higher likelihood that the murder took place there; low volumes can indicate that the victim was murdered in another location and dumped at our crime scene. Secondly, we removed all of the soil containing the remains and in the immediate vicinity of the remains in six bulk segments, as directed by Dr. Lubenski. Finally, we undertook an extensive mobile X-ray examination of the surrounding ground to check for more evidence. I can confirm that no other bones were discovered and no metal such as a revolver or bullet casings or fragments were identified. Of course you can fashion a deadly weapon with a good printer these days and paper or cardboard wouldn't show up, particularly in a decaying state, but we're not planning any further examinations on the site at this juncture unless instructed to'.

Hennessy was deciding whether or not to admonish Campbell for speaking out of turn when Lubenski came to her rescue.

'Thank you for that Ms. Campbell and for following the details of my request on removing all of that ground to the lab. It has arrived in our lab entirely as we wanted and I have two medical technicians processing it as we speak'.

'What does that involve exactly Oskar?' asked Hennessy, trying not to show the over-eagerness that he didn't appreciate in Campbell's response.

'Well, we start by taking dozens of photographs – I'm aware that STO Campbell's people did that on-site - so we know our starting point and then we basically attempt to extract the bones from the gravel as delicately as possible to ensure we don't break them or cause any further damage, inspect them for trauma, and then recreate the skeleton in the order that it's supposed to be in, in nature's order. Even the smallest fragment of bone could contain vital evidence, such as the perpetrator's DNA for example, so it's an intricate and time-consuming task but it's essential in this instance. And of course – '

'What about...sorry Oskar, please continue' interrupted Hennessy briefly, now feeling distinctly over-anxious.

'No problem Garoid' said Lubenski, sensing some tension in Hennessy's demeanour. 'We separate any clay on the individual bone parts using a special holding tank so that we don't lose any evidence of importance. In the case of what looks like dried blood, pieces of flesh or fragments of clothing, that is of course also carefully recorded and sent to the State Lab for testing. I thought initially that we might need a forensic anthropologist but I'm confident now we have the necessary skills here, both in our lab and a phone call away in the universities. We do however require a forensic entomologist as the high volume of insects in the soil may provide an indication of how long the victim has been dead for. I've invited a colleague of mine from Liverpool to join us and she arrives later today'.

'All going well, I expect the work to be largely completed' continued the pathologist quickly as he discerned another interruption from Hennessy, 'in the next two or three days'.

'Can I ask you Oskar' interjected AJ without interrupting Lubenski's flow, 'do you think you can extract DNA from the material you have or is our best chance of getting some sort of preliminary profile of the victim the samples that Aoife referenced?'

'Well, all of the samples go to the same lab for analysis AJ so hopefully between the two sets, we should get results that are useful to your investigation. I should add however that, like the rest of us, they are over-loaded with work at the moment so it may take a little while'.

'So when the results do come through' probed Hennessy, 'they may provide us with plenty of information to work on...gender...age range...height....maybe even identity if we're lucky and get a match on our databases?'

'We already know gender and age range Garoid, the skull and pelvic bones give us that: female in her sixties'.

Chapter 9

Hennessy was still digesting the implications of Lubenski's information when a sudden movement beside the entrance gate caught his attention.

Matt Griffin didn't look like a happy camper as he bounded over to the four people in the middle of the fill dump from the portable hut he emerged from, a span of about thirty metres. He was a muscular, fair-haired man in his late forties, and about one point eight metres high. His blue overalls and black boots had almost merged in colour and composition, blighted by years of wear, weather and muck. Two colourful tattoos adorned his neck: one of a serpent with its forked tongue sticking out, and the second of a sword facing downwards with a message in Latin wrapped around it. AJ had no doubt there were many more where they came from and expressed relief to herself that they were not on view, not from this distance at any rate. His gait could easily have been mistaken for a javelin thrower before they released the spear or a long distance jumper before they launched themselves into the air.

'For a start, you should all be wearing yellow jackets and hard hats, this is considered an active site by the Health and Safety Authority, we could be shut down!' stormed Griffin in a strong west of Ireland accent, stopping just short of knocking STO Campbell over.

'There's no equipment moving and there's no building activity above us that could land on our heads so let's drop all that bullshit. As for getting shut down, you don't have to worry about the Health and Safety Authority fella, I can do it right now' said an authoritative-sounding Hennessy.

'You've shut us down on-site already and I'm getting backed up with supplies, what the fuck is going on?' shouted Griffin, still radiating hostility.

'We're investigating a murder, that's what's fucking going on' responded Hennessy in a raised tone. 'Now, step at least two metres back from my colleague, drop the aggressive fucking attitude, and answer our questions before I arrest you for interfering with a murder case'.

'The fuck you will, I haven't done anything wrong' responded Griffin.

Both Hennessy and AJ – who now noticed that Griffin's hands were also covered in tattoos - had already concluded that the belligerent individual standing in front of them had a wealth of experience dealing with the officers of law enforcement previously, most likely including a judge or two. AJ decided that an alternative approach may yield a more fruitful outcome and she also didn't want Hennessy to have to carry out his ultimatum, an act that he would certainly have executed when she worked with him previously but whether or not he was that way inclined now, she wasn't sure.

'So how about we contact your boss and explain you're holding us up allowing work to restart on the runway?'

Griffin turned sharply to stare at AJ, trying but struggling to weigh her up.

'Why would you do that?' asked a slightly less confident Griffin after a pause.

'Because you are' said Hennessy.

Griffin maintained his hostile stance but his eyes showed that he was having a good think about his next move, a preoccupation that AJ believed he was less accustomed to.

'Can we move on?' asked Hennessy after another pause, noticing that AJ's question had dented Griffin's bluster. 'How does this fill dump operation work exactly: how do you know what they need on-site from day to day and how much do you record about where these piles of soil have come from and are going to?'

Griffin looked up at the sky for a short while before starting his answer, unsuccessfully concealing his retreat from Campbell's private space by pointing at the outer perimeter of the field.

'Everything from the back of the second hut to the fence in that direction is deliveries; everything else is back in from the site. I sign the deliveries in and tell the drivers where to unload, depending on what it is: gravel, clay, topsoil, the usual stuff. It doesn't spend long here, they only order in from suppliers when they need it. Those three mounds over there' continued Griffin pointing at three very large hills of material lying at the west end of the field, 'were delivered yesterday and supposed to go on-site this morning. I have a record of what's delivered and what's called to the site so I know what stock we have here at any point'.

'What about the soil that's trucked here from the site and then back in again; that takes up about what, a third of this field?' asked AJ.

'Yeah, that doesn't happen on most big sites but these guys are big into tidiness. Records are much looser for that stuff because it's already been paid for plus the drivers are working for us so they know what they're at. Is that it, can I get back to work now? asked Griffin, getting bolshie again.

'So you work for the company building the runway, who else works with you?' probed Hennessy.

'Yes and nobody. There's security here twenty-four-seven, uses the same hut as me, the other one has high-value stuff, mainly electrical equipment and parts' answered Griffin pointing at the second hut beside the entrance.

'And who do you report to?' queried AJ.

'Says in my contract the two project managers but any of the supervisors can order from me, so long as I get the email I'm happy. No paperwork here, it's all on tablets they give us; something to do with the environment and some fucking stupid medal they got'.

The last bit didn't make sense to AJ but Hennessy got in before she could follow up.

'I heard about that. Do you record where exactly on the construction site the soil here is going to and coming from?

'Don't know, don't care, couldn't give a shite' replied a smiling Griffin, at least one front tooth distinctly missing, and not from natural causes AJ was surmising.

'Has there ever been any break-ins here, any damage to the front gate, that kind of thing?' queried AJ.

'A few times the equipment hut was damaged by fuckers trying to break in, stupid bollox security guys were asleep next door, but nothing was ever taken'.

'You must have got them on the cameras?' asked Hennessy.

'Yip but they were wearing hoodies and it was pitch dark, no floodlights here on account of the fucking useless security guards. In any ways, they never took anything'.

'Did you report those incidents to us?' asked AJ.

'Reported them to my bosses, nothing to do with me after that. Are we done?' said Griffin starting to walk away.

'What about break-ins where they left stuff here or threw it over the fence: stolen cars, mobile phones, shovels, maybe earth moved where they were burying something, anything like that?' asked Hennessy.

'If you're asking me if some stupid fuckers topped someone here or dumped a body here when there's cameras all over the place, and a security guy in the hut supposed to be awake and doing patrols every hour, you must be fucking joking? Now, I'm done answering your dopey fucking questions, arrest me or call my boss, I couldn't give two fucks' said Griffin striding back towards the hut he came from.

'There is one more thing' said Hennessy in a raised tone to make sure that Griffin heard him, 'this site is a potential crime scene and I'm closing it, with immediate effect'.

Chapter 10

Only two people knew its location.

Fran Balfe was in reflective mood as he ambled around the small, dark shop in the south county Dublin village of Killiney. It was his wife's idea to open a small business when she retired after thirty five years as a general practitioner. Although neither had previous experience in the retail business, it didn't take long for the couple to agree on an area that they had both been taking an increasing interest in at the time. From period furniture to paintings to furniture to books to fine china and even writing instruments, they had been collecting antiques since shortly after they were married.

Seventeen kilometres south of Dublin city centre, Killiney was where his wife had grown up and where they had moved to when she retired. That was nearly five years ago now and more than three years since they had converted the ground floor into *Village Antiques*. Their initial stock consisted of various pieces they had collected themselves but no longer wanted but his wife took to travelling around the country and returning home with 'bargains'. It soon transpired that shop-keepers they were not and whilst they enjoyed cleaning, polishing and presenting their wares, the business side of things was often neglected or deliberately avoided in the case of his wife. There again, profit was never the motive as he had a very comfortable pension from his career as an engineer and his wife's long service to the country's health system had also proved lucrative. It was more of a hobby with modest financial benefits that they had embarked upon.

    The blinds on the three large windows at the front of the shop were always closed in order to prevent unwanted prying eyes and the result was a dark interior, even with the lights on. Large pieces such as furniture were displayed in the centre of the store with smaller objects such as porcelain and jewellery exhibited in glass cases, some of which were locked. All of the paintings and some of the rugs were hung on three of the walls with the larger or more expensive items highlighted with spotlights. Prices were discretely attached to everything but, as is standard in the industry, were always negotiable.

Although the front door had a typed notice with opening times, they were more indicative than actual and interested customers tended to ring the doorbell if the shop was closed. In fact their rather lacklustre approach to abiding by the stated opening hours had proved quite efficient at keeping time-wasting browsers away.

Sales were few and far between for the first few years and when the Covid pandemic hit, they were forced to close. That was what prompted Fran to use his experience of technology to set up a website. Within a few weeks, international collectors began to take an interest. So much so that Fran's wife expanded her sales trips to spend several weeks at a time, exploring antique shows and markets in the United States and Asia. During such trips she would become so engrossed in her purchasing exploits that Fran might not hear from her for weeks at a time. Although she had a mobile phone, she rarely turned it on and, when tackled by Fran about being so difficult to contact, complained that she needed to focus on the business at hand rather than fuss over technology that she neither liked nor fully understood.

Once he got so worried about her when hearing of a mass shooting in a shopping mall in Portsmouth, New Hampshire that he rang hotels in the city trying to find her. He knew that she had travelled to New Hampshire and loved touring around its many renowned antiques centres but whether she was in Portsmouth or in a shopping mall in Portsmouth he had no idea. As her passport was in her maiden name, Rebecca Cohen, but often made hotel reservations in her married name, reception staff quickly tired of his enquiries about a golden-ager who might be staying under one of two names. Citing guest privacy policies, several hotels had explained that they could not divulge such information but undertook to leave a message if she was a guest. A week later Rebecca arrived home with two suitcases full of purchases and dismissed Fran's protestations about her lack of communication claiming that he was overreacting and that she was 'no where near Portsmouth at the time'. Several subsequent entreaties to his wife met with similar negative responses as the travel pattern continued: a large withdrawal of cash from their business account, several weeks of silence, and suitcases full of purchases on return.

Fran was responsible for cataloguing, photographing and listing the antiques but he relied on his wife to price them as there were little or no receipts. When he attempted to establish procurement price details from Rebecca, she either maintained the article in question was bought from a car boot sale with no paperwork or, occasionally, produce a handwritten receipt on a piece of crumpled paper. On one such occasion, the crumpled up receipt was on a 'Dino's Diner, Northwood, NH' serviette. Reassuring customers of the provenance of said items, however, never seemed to be an issue, much to Fran's surprise.

The nature of his wife's purchases also surprised her husband, providing him with considerable curiosity and amusement. One such item was a hand-towel sized Persian rug which his wife said cost US$500 and should be priced at Eur3000. There was no paperwork with it but his wife assured him that discerning buyers would have no difficulty accepting its bone fides when they felt its quality and saw its artistry. It was sold within a week.

Not all transactions were as profitable however. On one sales trip his wife paid US$800 for a Limited Edition 888 rose gold Montblanc fountain pen in Hong Kong and listed it at Eur6000. After several weeks of inquiries and shop visits, Rebecca eventually concluded that it was indeed a genuine Montblanc writing instrument but a 'Special' Edition version and worth about Eur700. They both agreed the best course of action would be to remove it from their listing and keep it for use as a birthday or Christmas present for a relative. It was still in their safe as Fran continued his stroll around the shop, stopping regularly to inspect and reminisce about certain products. He dusted as he went as cleanliness was a top priority, taking particular care with a nineteenth century satinwood Carlton house desk, priced at Eur11500. When the top was gleaming, he carefully opened each of the five mahogany drawers underneath and shined them, along with their engraved brass handles.

As he unlatched the casing to adjust the hands on a Caseway grandfather clock that they purchased at Portobello road market in London before they started their own business, he smiled when he recalled the debate they had about the definition of an antique. Fran was firmly of the view that the hundred year rule applied but Rebecca had her own interpretation: 'a collectible object whose age and quality made it valuable'. To Fran, that meant 'vintage' not 'antique'. The discussion continued over their dinner in an Italian restaurant in Camden that evening and by 10 pm they concluded that both perspectives would apply to their own business, should they ever launch one. They paid Stg£2000 and priced it at Eur3000 but it remained unsold. Rebecca had often suggested lowering the price to get rid of it but Fran had a soft spot for it, something about its elegance and stature comforted him. And after all, they had acquired it for their own collection, not for resale purposes.

When Fran reached the shop's oak wood counter with its National cash register, he was reflecting on another, more recent, debate with his wife, one that did not end in agreement. It concerned an object that Rebecca had brought back from a buying trip to Thailand and Malaysia, although the piece itself was Chinese in origin. Most unusually, Rebecca opened one of her bags as soon as she arrived home and took out a heavily wrapped item, explaining as she revealed it that it was a Chinese porcelain vase with a carved dragon, possibly one of a set. Dating back to the eighteenth century, it stood about thirty centimetres in height and, as Rebecca understood, was worth at least ten times the US$500 she purported to have paid for it in Bangkok's Chatuchak weekend market. Fran's discomfort was further exacerbated when she refused to have it listed in their catalogue, stating that she wanted to hold on to it for a while until she checked something out. She wouldn't even agree to store it in the safe, which was fitted with a monitored alarm. The more questions Fran asked – staring uneasily at the figure's piercing, fearsome gaze - the more evasive his wife became. All would be clarified she explained, when she returned from another trip, which started the next day.

That was the last exchange they had had thought Fran as he wiped some dust off the top of the cash register, and that was almost six weeks ago.

Chapter 11

'Fuck him and the horse he rode in on'.

Hennessy was briefing DS Brophy in her Garda HQ office in the Phoenix Park when she reacted negatively to the complaint he relayed from the Irish Project Manager of Spire Limited.

Most of the senior officers in the Criminal Investigation Department of the Garda National Bureau of Criminal Investigation were based at Harcourt Square in Dublin city centre but Brophy had managed to hold on to her Phoenix Park office by saying that she was retiring shortly and that younger officers should get priority for the limited office space in Harcourt Square. In reality, she hated traffic and few streets in Dublin had busier traffic than Harcourt Street. Accessing and parking HQ in the Phoenix Park was a lot easier. The office was on the second floor in the north-east corner, overlooking one of the many staff car parks. Although the windows had been renovated, the rest of the furnishings looked inexpensive and old. Brophy's light brown rectangular desk was beside the only window and beside the door a few metres away was a small square maple wood meeting table with four brown, fake leather chairs, one of which Hennessy was sitting on. Three framed drawings hung on the walls, one a portrait of an un-named woman and the other two struck Hennessy as images from the surrounding park. He couldn't see any attempts by Brophy to personalise or soften her workplace: no family photographs, no fresh flowers, not even a colourful calendar.

'The technical staff say they need a few days to fully examine the fill site but I should be able to let them back on the main construction site later today or first thing in the morning' said Hennessy.

'Have you told him about letting him back on the main site?' probed Brophy.

'Not yet ma'am'.

'Good, call me an old termagant Detective Inspector but in my opinion people who put their own interests ahead of a homicide inquiry evince a distinct apathetic lack of empathy' replied Brophy.

Hennessy didn't respond.

'So we have one or two crime scenes, a victim in her sixties, and....forgive me for being a curmudgeon here Detective...what else?' asked Brophy.

'Detective Jenkinson has started looking at the CCTV footage but it's very difficult to know what we're looking for or over what period. If the autopsy can narrow the time of death window and if we can establish a transport mode for disposing of the remains where we found them, we should be in a better position' explained Hennessy, even though he had no idea what termagant meant.

'But we are one hundred percent certain that death was by bullet?' probed Brophy.

'That's the pathologist's initial assumption ma'am, which we're still working under but we're probably up to a week away from having a definitive cause of death'.

'Can't those medical folk use their legerdemain to move more briskly?' probed Brophy.

'I'll contact them again ma'am but they're working on quite a few cases at the moment, as you know', again trying not to show his ignorance of the big word.

'Indeed Detective, murders in this country have taken on a much more amorphous nature in recent times. I wince when I reflect on the sheer volume of unhinged fuckers with a concupiscence for violence nowadays; it bespeaks of a partial breakdown in societal values I believe. Forgive my misophonic soliloquy but I'm looking forward to issuing a valedictory salute to crime and assuming Goblin-mode' said Brophy.

Hennessy was pretty sure Brophy was referencing her much-rumoured retirement as he struggled to unpack her speech but he wasn't about to seek clarification.

'We've also established ma'am that relations between the Irish and Spanish workers on the site may not always have been cordial, a little fractious at times we understand' said Hennessy.

'Construing its significance as...?' queried Brophy.

'We're not sure yet ma'am but it may prove relevant as we progress the investigation' answered Hennessy in a hopeful tone.

There was a pause as Brophy reflected on how limited the progress was so far.

'I may be able to chime a tintinnabulation of hope on your inquiry Garoid: I have been able to appoint another detective to your team'.

Chapter 12

After almost twenty years experience, Norman Prendergast had conducted hundreds of Fine Art auctions but he had to admit that the pandemic had brought online viewing and bidding to a whole new level.

When he left school he had no intention of going to college so tried various hospitality jobs before heading off on his own to travel around South America, initially for three months. His foster parents – who had adopted him as a toddler - advised against it but he loved the outdoors and figured trekking across the Andes for a few months would be good for his mental and physical health. Two years later and a lean, bronzed, fair haired, one hundred and eighty centimetres tall, twenty-one year old arrived back in

Wexford town and informed his foster parents that he had chosen his career path: fine arts and antiquities.

The interest arose, he explained to them, when he arrived in Machu Picchu, an eight kilometre long fifteenth century Incan citadel located high in the Andes Mountains in Peru. He was fascinated both by the sophistication of that civilisation and by the artefacts excavated at the site when it was 'rediscovered' by Hiram Bingham in 1911, chronicling the find in his book: The Lost City of the Incas'. Settling in to a student hostel in the nearby city of Cusco for over a month, Norman had undertaken the seven hour, seventy two kilometre train journey to the site on an almost daily basis to marvel at its wonders. Although most of the artefacts had been shipped by Bingham to Yale University for more detailed study, he was able to see and admire some of the 46,000 pieces in the University of Cusco. Such was his interest, Norman had returned to Peru in 2012 to view the then repatriated pieces at the Casa Concha Museum in Cusco, taking a particular shine to the silver statues and ceramic vessels.

Between his first and second visits, Norman had successfully completed a Diploma in Fine and Decorative Arts at the Institute of Professional

Auctioneers and Valuers and a four-year Bachelor of Arts Degree in Fine Art at what was to become the Technological University of Dublin. After two short but enjoyable stints at small antiques' shops on Dublin's Francis Street, he took out a loan, rented a derelict premises on Bridgefoot Street beside the river Liffey, and opened 'Prendergast's Fine Art and Antiquities'.

Engaged twice but never married, he lived on his own in an apartment overlooking the river midway between his shop and Guinness' St. James Gate brewery. The brewery and its surrounding public houses had most likely contributed to his more stout appearance in recent times but his receding hairline he could only put down to age, with a few years to go before he hit fifty. Dressed in his customary tailored navy suit, he was now preparing to start an auction at 2pm on Wednesday July 21st, 2021. Although selling was one of four inter-related roles he played – the others being valuing, managing, and purchasing – it was his favourite. Feeling the buzz of the live auction room and watching the psychology underpinning the bidding process play out gave him great satisfaction in his career choice. During lockdowns, the online-only auctions were cold, lifeless and clinical in his opinion.

Today, there were fifteen real collectors in his auction room, even though the Covid pandemic was still at large and so the rules regarding mask-wearing and social-distancing had to be adhered to. In addition, eighteen other parties had registered to participate in the online element. Who exactly these latter individuals were was difficult to tell as collectors regularly used friends, legal firms or family members to complete the registration formalities. He wasn't about to enforce strict identification procedures as plenty of genuine collectors had legitimate reasons to conduct their buying and selling activities in a confidential manner; they also had a lot of funds. He recognised almost all of the participants and could tell in most cases which items each was interested in.

Prior to any auction, Prendergast would discuss and agree valuations for the items to be auctioned with their owners or agents. Many relied on his skill and experience in assessing age, condition, origin and quality in order to set a reserve price but several customers insisted on specifying the minimum amount that they would accept. In this particular auction, there were twenty-seven lots, three-quarters of which he had valued. The theme of the auction was

Asian Art and included Chinese jades, Korean ceramics, and several early Buddhist sculptures from Japan, one of which had been repaired using the Kintsugi method. This 'golden joinery' approach to mending pottery and sculptures used a lacquer mixed with powdered gold, believing that breakage was part of the piece's history and should therefore not be disguised, asserting that the gold element made the piece stronger after the repair.

The auction room itself was deliberately decorated in strong, vibrant colours to make participants feel energy in the room, and anti-glare, task lighting to focus attention on each lot as it was presented for sale. The seating was designed to provide comfort but, given the age profile of the buyers, not sufficient comfort to fall asleep. As a smiling Prendergast stepped up to the podium, he knew that his job was to keep energy levels high in the room by moving quickly and enthusiastically through the catalogue, and to imbue a certain cheerfulness into the proceedings by using humour as and when he deemed appropriate.

'Good afternoon ladies and gentlemen and welcome to our live auction of rare and exquisite pieces of fine art. My name is Norman Prendergast and I will be your auctioneer for the sale of the twenty seven lots listed in our catalogue'.

It was exactly 2pm on Prendergast's Omega Seamaster watch.

The process followed a standard format: each lot was introduced with a description of the item or items on offer, their provenance explained, and offers invited starting at a certain amount of money.

By 2.30pm, business was moving swiftly with twelve lots sold and two withdrawn for failing to meet their reserve amounts. The prices being achieved were more or less in line with Prendergast's expectations, as were the number and identity of bidders making successful offers. Lot number thirteen however was what his attention was particularly drawn to this afternoon. It was described by its seller as a Japanese Buddhist porcelain vase containing a significant volume of twenty-four-Karat gold leaves but Prendergast believed that it had been repaired in Japan but was in fact originally from China and that it was one of a set of two. Individually, the two pieces were valuable in their own right but combined they were worth considerably more. He had deliberately positioned the item halfway through the auction to allow him sufficient opportunity to gauge the identity and mood of the bidders who were in buying mode. More importantly, he was focused on the collector sitting three seats from the back on his left-hand side. In his late sixties, short-ish, with greying hair and wearing a black fedora hat, he was nicknamed 'Klondike' for his love of antiques containing gold, particularly from Asia.

Prendergast made a point of emphasising that he was using the vendor's description when introducing lot number thirteen as one of his assistants moved it from a wooden desk at the side of the room to the display stand in front of the podium. Prendergast knew that the spotlight over the display stand would highlight the gold leaves in the Kintsugi-repaired piece. What he did not know was if anyone present or online was aware of the origin of the vase or the existence of its sister piece as only very careful inspection and research would reveal same. Some purists would always consider a repaired item, no matter how valuable or containing how much gold, to be just that: broken but others thought of the Kintsugi method to be value-enhancing rather than destroying. Much would be revealed thought Prendergast as he invited bids starting at nine thousand Euro.

Silence in an auction room when first offers were invited was nothing new, regardless of what was being sold. Rather than indicating that no one was interested, it often signalled significant interest but also significant psychology at work as bidders waited to see who would go first and how quickly their arm went up. Prendergast waited the customary ten seconds or so as he closely observed the key players and then tried to stoke up more enthusiasm by energetically cajoling his audience to reflect on the rarity and artistry of the vase. He then added some humour by suggesting that the sheer volume of gold leaves alone were worth the nine thousand Euro.

After another five seconds a hand was raised but its source surprised the auctioneer. It was a bid from one of the online buyers, communicated by the staff member monitoring the remote-registered customer, and it was in the amount of eight thousand seven hundred and fifty Euro.

'Thank you to number forty three for starting us off. Now ladies and gentleman, you couldn't possibly allow such a valuable item to be snapped up for such a bargain price, can I invite more reasonable offers please?'

Seven more bids were made within the next thirty seconds, four increasing the price by two hundred and fifty Euro each, one by one hundred Euro, one by fifty Euro, and the seventh one by three hundred Euro. Silence again descended on the room after the brief flurry of activity, with the highest offer now standing at ten thousand two hundred Euro. The energy in the room was now replaced by a certain level of nervousness as buyers paused to take stock of the proceedings they had just witnessed and as Prendergast waved both of his arms excitedly to encourage to whip up more bids.

Several seconds passed before a tall blonde lady in her forties wearing a crimson woollen overcoat raised her left hand holding a white card showing buyer number thirty eight, and calmly offered eleven thousand Euro.

Often referred to in the trade as the 'kill' bid, Prendergast turned towards the woman whose first and only bid of the entire afternoon raised the price by eight hundred Euro. He didn't recognise her. In fact, he hadn't even noticed her before now, even though she was sitting in the front row. A black face mask with a small white logo in one corner was pulled under her chin, revealing bright red lipstick. The woman's facial expression was poker-like, displaying no giveaway signs of being serious or uncertain or mischievous. He was aware of dummy bidders being deployed by some unscrupulous sellers to make fake offers in order to drive the price up but not at this price-level.

After a brief pause, Prendergast held his gavel out towards the previous highest bidder.

'Eleven thousand Euro to you Sir, can you make it eleven thousand two hundred, still a bargain Sir?'

Klondike kept his hand down and nodded a negative, disappointed response.

'Anyone else ladies and gentlemen, eleven thousand two hundred for this unique piece?' pleased Prendergast.

No reply.

'Going once, going twice to number thirty eight in the front row ladies and gentlemen, any increase on eleven thousand Euro?'

Silence.

'Sold, to number thirty eight for eleven thousand Euro'.

There was a short period of feet shuffling and seat adjusting amongst the audience as lot thirteen was removed from the display stand and replaced by two smaller wooden items comprising lot number fourteen.

Prendergast continued on with the auction but couldn't help taking obvious and more surreptitious glances at the lady in the front seat. How come he didn't know her? Was she taking instructions from a third party through her phone or a hidden earpiece under her hair? Why did she only make one bid during the entire auction? If she only attended for one item, why didn't she pay for it and leave immediately afterwards? He was trying to remember if she had an accent when she made the offer as he continued on with the remaining fourteen lots. As far as he could recall amidst the adrenaline rush that he still got when nearing a sale, there was no discernible modulation or intonation in the two words that she uttered. The more he attempted to re-focus on the business to hand, the more his mind went back to her. Discombobulated was the term that came to mind that best described his feelings as he pondered the questions he had asked himself but he knew he couldn't make it obvious, he had to maintain a professional demeanour.

Buyer number thirty eight remained almost motionless for the next sixty five minutes, exhibiting little or no interest in buying anything else.

When proceedings had ended and Prendergast thanked everyone for attending, he headed straight for his office and rang his accountant at the sales desk where successful bidders were paying for their purchases. He had to find out more about buyer number thirty eight, ideally a name and address so that he could conduct more research into her.

His motive was simple: he was intent on stealing lot number thirteen from whomever bought it.

Chapter 13

The Airport Police Control Centre had three mask-wearing officers gathered around a screen when AJ went back to learn and watch more about the positioning of cameras at the runway construction site.

'It's the parallax effect isn't it?' asked one of the officers as she leaned closer to the screen.

'Looks like it' replied the other officer.

AJ could see from the monitor they were both examining that it was a view of part of the boundary fence and decided to ask what the parallax effect is.

'It's to do with an object appearing to be in a different position when we study it from two different positions; in our case, that usually means two different CCTV cameras' explained the female officer. 'So what seems to be a cardboard box lying against the boundary fence near Gate 42 is beside a fence post on one camera but not so near the fence on another'.

'Does that make a huge difference?' probed AJ.

'Not so much with a stationary object like a cardboard box but if we see somebody trying to intrude on to the airfield, it's very important that we dispatch our patrols to the right location' clarified the officer. 'Anyway, you're here to talk about the camera positions over at the runway construction site?' queried the same member of the Airport Police.

'Exactly, I was here before but I understand that the spots for the cameras can change as the construction goes on, is that the case?'

'Yeah, we may move positions for a few reasons. For example, if the boundary gate the builders are using for access changes or if there's a lot of expensive equipment being parked near a particular part of the fence' explained the officer.

'That makes sense. So tell me, do you keep records of all of the camera positions since construction began?' probed AJ.

'Absolutely, we keep a log of them on our system. I can print it out for you or email it if that'd be easier?'

As AJ was giving the officer her Garda email address, her mobile phone rang.

It was Hennessy.

'AJ, I'm in the airport station. I want to introduce you to our new team member'.

Chapter 14

'Hundred percent Boss'.

'Romance fraud?'

'Hundred percent'.

'To homicide?'

'Well, a lot of murders involve lovers Boss, crimes of passion if you will'.

'So they say. Anyway, welcome to the team John' said Hennessy.

'Actually Boss, my middle name is James so they call me...'

'No!' interrupted Hennessy abruptly, 'we're not calling you JJ, we've already got an AJ on the team for fuck's sake. We'll call you Johnny'.

Newly promoted Detective John James Lennon remained motionless and speechless in his seat in the Airport Garda Station conference room. He watched an aircraft with an entirely white livery march slowly past the window behind his new boss, Detective Inspector Garoid Hennessy. Lennon was shorter than Hennessy, about one hundred and seventy-seven centimetres, but looked leaner and fitter. He was twenty-eight years old, had reddish-brown hair, and was dressed in a smart casual way: black slacks, black leather shoes, light blue shirt and navy light coat.

Hennessy took out files from his brief case and commenced the task of bringing Lennon up to speed on the investigation to date, a task that he felt shouldn't take that long. After about fifteen minutes of updating, questions and answers, another team member entered the conference room.

'Hi, I'm AJ' she smiled as she took off her sunglasses and sat down four places away from the new recruit.

'I'm - '

'Detective Garda Johnny Lennon' interrupted Hennessy.

'Please to meet you' continued Lennon a little nervously.

'Welcome aboard. How long have you been a detective?' queried AJ as she removed her face mask.

'Eh...a few months'.

'Good for you. Where did you work before?' probed AJ.

Lennon was about to answer when the Station Sergeant, Tim Coady, knocked and entered the room.

'AJ, we've got a runner in Terminal 1 and I'm short-staffed, would you?' asked Coady before looking at Hennessy. 'Sorry Gar, d'ya mind if I borrow her, she knows the lie of the land around here?'

'What the fuck is a runner?' exclaimed Hennessy in response.

'Someone being extradited who makes a run for it when they get to the airport' explained Coady.

'Sure' said Hennessy looking at AJ, who was getting up from her seat. 'And take Johnny with you'.

AJ was using the airport radio set that Coady had given her to get more information as she hurried into the Arrivals Floor of Terminal 1, Johnny Lennon tagging along behind her.

'Would they not be in handcuffs?' asked Lennon as he caught up with her on the escalator to the Departures Floor.

'Usually, but they might have asked the escorts to remove them to use the toilet or something' explained AJ.

'Who are the escorts?' probed Lennon.

'Two guards from the Extradition Department in Phoenix Park. They assess the request to remove handcuffs based on how likely an escape would be'.

'I see, so the strength of the guy, what he's being extradited for, his attitude, et cetera?'

'Didn't you hear the comms?' asked AJ as she showed her Garda ID to get through security screening. 'The escapee is a female'.

When they arrived at security screening AJ showed her Garda ID and alerted the staff that she was armed so the metal detector would be triggered. Lennon held up his ID and said he wasn't armed. AJ noticed a small tattoo of an eagle on the underside of his right hand.

'Is it that big a deal, I mean they can't really get far?' asked Lennon as they turned right after screening.

'It is if they get on to the airfield, could close the airport until they're back in custody' clarified AJ.

Several more communications took place on the radio set before AJ and Lennon arrived at the location where the escapee was last seen, adjacent to Gate B140. One of the two escort officers was present along with two members of the Airport Police.

'She wanted to go to the loo so we took off her cuffs' said the female escort officer after hurried introductions, beckoning to the toilets situated directly behind the retail outlet.

'Did you go in with her?' probed AJ.

'No, we stayed here; where could she go?'

'Well she obviously went somewhere. Where's the other escort?' said AJ.

'He's double-checking the men's toilet to make sure she didn't slip in there'.

'Have you done extraditions before?' probed AJ looking around.

'He has, it's my first' answered the female escort officer, referring to her absent colleague.

There was a pause in the conversation as the public address system announced a change of departure gate for Ryanair's flight to Krakow. Several hundred departing passengers were in the immediate area which contained twelve boarding gates and AJ quickly realised that the throng of people rushing by, many wheeling suitcases, most donning face masks, made a challenging situation even more complex.

'We're checking the CCTV and we have four patrols on the airfield; we've a good description so shouldn't take too long till she's spotted' said one of the two airport police officers.

'Good, I suggest you both start at the end of the pier, we'll start here, and we'll meet up somewhere in the middle, does that sound okay?' suggested AJ, conscious that the airport police don't have to take instructions from Gardaí.

'Sure, we'll let Control know'.

The male Extradition officer emerged from the toilets area as the two airport police officers. He had a sheepish expression as he approached AJ and Lennon.

'Ryan, Extradition Unit, there's no sign in the men's or invalid toilets, no clothes dumped in cubicles or bins, she must be wearing the same ones'.

'What if she swapped outfits with someone waiting for her?' queried AJ in an irritated tone.

'Hardly' said Ryan with a bemused look.

'What do you mean 'hardly' for fuck's sake? Do you realise how much trouble you've caused here, how many resources have been deployed to sort out your fucking mistake? What if she runs across the runway when a plane is landing, what if she assaults someone to get away? What's she getting extradited for anyway?'

'Eh...she's wanted in Romania I think it is' answered Ryan.

'Attempted murder in Bulgaria' corrected his female colleague.

'Jesus!' blurted out AJ, staring angrily at Ryan.

Ryan peered at Lennon, as if for some male support, and then looked down at his feet.

'You two take the right-hand side, we'll take the left. Check every single individual, male and female, every toilet, every bar, every coffee shop, and every staff area. Take a note of any door that's locked, we'll get someone with a master key to open them. Clear?' asked AJ in a stern tone, indicating to Lennon and the female escort officer.

As soon as they were out of ear shot of their two colleagues, AJ tuned brusquely to Ryan.

'Okay, tell me exactly what fucking happened, no more bullshit'.

'Like I said – '

'Were you in the bar when she went missing?' shouted AJ.

'No, Christ!' said Ryan slightly panicked.

AJ continued staring.

'I was in the men's when she went missing, I told Grainne to take off the cuffs and let her go to the toilet. I didn't know she'd – '

'You fucking idiot, you let a rookie make decisions. How long were you gone?' snapped AJ.

Ryan was looking down at his feet again.

'How fucking long Ryan?'

'About fifteen minutes' whispered Ryan.

'Were you shooting up?' probed AJ quickly.

'No...I was...reading sports stories on the phone, you can check it' answered a defensive Ryan.

As Ryan waited for another rebuke, AJ dramatically pushed him aside and sprinted across the corridor.

Ryan turned in time to see his escortee standing over a prone figure at the outer edge of the Shamrock bar. She was brandishing a shiny silver knife and the person on the ground was Lennon.

Chapter 15

It was just after 3am when the two figures approached the back of the house, one of four in a quiet cul-de-sac off Santry Avenue, midway between Dublin Airport and the city centre. They had driven past it earlier in the evening and couldn't see any intruder alarm boxes or external cameras. The houses on either side however did have alarm boxes over the front doors and one had a 'Beware of Dog' notice attached to the entrance gate. Each of the four bungalows was surrounded by two metre high brick walls, with metal vehicle gates at the front and wooden pedestrian gates at the rear.

There was a full moon and very few clouds which didn't help the plan of the two men as they crept along the overgrown, unlit pathway until they reached the second house. One of the men then hunched down and lifted his colleague high enough to see into the back garden. They were of similar size and frame, and dressed in black pullovers, combat trousers, gloves, and balaclavas. After observing the three houses that he could see for several minutes, he lifted himself on to the top of the wall. There were no internal lights on, no cameras or kennels that he could spot, and no motion sensor lights. He turned sideways and lifted the first man on to the wall, then both lowered themselves onto an unkempt lawn. Again, they hunkered down and remained as motionless as possible for several minutes before creeping along the fifteen metres of grass using the shadow of the side wall as cover - to the back door. To an observer their movements seemed almost choreographed such was the smoothness and calmness of their motion. No words were exchanged between them, only glances.

Half of the white upvc door consisted of a frosted glass window. One of the men reached into the top side pocket of his combats and withdrew a silver, folding pick lock. Within a minute he had opened the lock and was slowly pushing down the handle when he stopped and looked at his colleague. They both knew what action to take if they triggered an alarm or woke a dog. He gently pushed the door until it was about fifteen centimetres wide.

Nothing.

As both men stood up, the one who picked the lock returned the tool to his pocket and reassured himself by briefly holding the leather sheath of his ten centimetre long, double-sided, hunting knife.

They both pushed the door wide open, stepped into the dark kitchen, and closed it behind them. There was very little light coming in the main window but neither man carried a torch, finding them a high-risk hindrance too often in the past. The sink and food preparation area were located in front of the back window whilst the cooking and refrigeration equipment was positioned along the wall to their right.

They didn't know the layout of the house or number of occupants before they entered. It didn't really concern them. They were singularly focussed on the task in hand.

The door into the hallway - held open with a doorstop - had four doors off it, all white and all closed. They walked halfway along the corridor on a dark, firm carpet until they could just make out an open-plan dining / living room at the far end, looking out on to the front garden. Both men instinctively concluded that the four doors probably had three bedrooms and a bathroom behind them. One of the men beckoned to the other to follow him into the dining / living room. They systematically moved around the rectangular room – one on either side – checking the visible items and searching for a safe or locked cabinets where valuable items might be stored out of sight. At one point car headlights appeared outside and they stooped below the level of the window until they heard a door open and footsteps move away from their bungalow. One of the men peeped out from behind the window curtain when the headlights were moving around the turning circle in the cul-de-sac and monitored the taxi as it drove off.

There were a number of display stands, cupboards, and large paintings in the room and the men took their time meticulously inspecting each one. The streetlight on the road in front of the house just about provided sufficient illumination for them to conduct their activities efficiently. Any item of interest was closely scrutinised to assess its similarity with the photograph which they had been provided with earlier that day. None matched and there was no indication of a safe or hidden cabinet. In fact - to their admittedly untrained eyes - the furniture and contents of this house struck them as cheap, old and worthless. As they finished their search around the sides of the room, they moved to the large dining table in the middle of it. Scratches and stains were clearly visible even in the dim lighting. There were four candlesticks, two small statues, and two larger bowls. None were of interest to the two intruders.

Several opened letters were left on the table in front of a fragile-looking chair. One man flicked through them and picked up one that had 'final reminder' emblazoned across the middle, underlined and in bold capitals. He held it up until he could read the first paragraph.

This is a final warning that your rent has not been paid for two months and, unless full payment is received by this office within forty-eight hours of the date stamp above, a **Notice of Termination** *to vacate the property will be issued, in accordance with your Lease and the rules of the Residential Tenancies Board.*

When he first started plying this trade many years ago, he would ponder the inconsistency between the merchandise he was in search of and the plight of the people who had said merchandise – if only temporarily - in their possession. Time and experience, however, rendered him no longer curious enough to engage in such futile endeavours. Nowadays, he was more concerned with successfully accomplishing the assigned mission as speedily and efficiently as possible; he had his reputation to consider. He showed the letter to his fellow burglar, nodded, left it back on the table, and walked purposefully back in to the hall. No words were needed to communicate their next steps.

When they carefully turned the black aluminium door handle of the first door and inched it slightly open, they were met with total darkness. One of the men stuck his head in and quickly recognised that the window had blackout curtains. What little light there was in the hall struggled to project itself into the room and hence the men found it very difficult to discern its nature, layout and occupancy. While one stood outside the door to monitor any unwanted activity, the other got down on his hands and knees and slowly slithered into the blackness in snake-like fashion. In less than a minute, he had established that it was an empty single bedroom.

The second door was only a few centimetres ajar when they could distinguish striped tiling on the floor. The unpleasant odour that promptly followed confirmed that it was a toilet.

As they approached the final two rooms, one on either side of the hallway, they heard what sounded like the click of a light switch accompanied almost instantaneously by a faint brightness sneaking out from under the door to their right. They quickly assumed squatting positions on either side of the door.

'What's wrong?'

'Too much alcohol tonight, I need to – '

'Turn off the fucking light!'

The two intruders glanced at one another, both quickly recognising that their Plan B was going to be deployed sooner than they had expected.

The man on the same side of the door handle took two steps backwards as he stood up, indicating that he would deal with the remaining occupant when the first emerged into the hall.

His colleague stood up and reached in to his pocket for his trusty hunting knife.

Chapter 16

The phone call from Lubenski didn't surprise Hennessy as he waited for his two team members to return from their search for the runner. He had been expecting an update any day.

'Hi Gar, thought I'd give you some preliminary results, report will follow later as usual' said Lubenski.

'Thanks Oskar, go ahead' answered a relieved yet anxious Hennessy.

'I've spoken to the technician involved, Campbell as well, so some of these points are partly hers or corroborated by her' explained the pathologist.

'A couple of headline findings to get out of the way first: it's definitely a bullet wound in the woman's skull, probably nine millimetre calibre, but we didn't find any fragments. Based on the position of entry and angle of trajectory, it was almost certainly fatal. Next, all of the bones found were from one individual so it wasn't a mass grave, as a few sensationalist newspapers suggested. Also, that fill dump where they store materials for the main construction site; we found no trace evidence there, so we're dealing with one crime scene'.

'Was that the murder scene?' asked Hennessy.

'Unlikely. For two reasons: the volume of blood that we estimated from what we collected around the remains isn't consistent with the expected blood loss from the gunshot. Secondly, my entomologist friend examined the insect activity on the remains and in the surrounding clay and considers that the body was there for a number of days, a week at most' explained Lubenski.

'Why couldn't she have been murdered there in the last week?' probed Hennessy.

'That brings us to the stage of decomposition of the body. The advanced stage that we found the remains in is not consistent with the bugs found and the state of the soft tissue inside the bones, the marrow'.

'Which means?' queried Hennessy.

'We're still waiting for more advanced test results to come back from the State Lab but it seems to point to the dead body experiencing conditions that accelerated its decay. The three main ways to achieve this are some combination of high temperatures, water and humidity' said Lubenski.

'So you think whoever killed her deliberately wanted her to decay quicker? Why, to erase evidence?'

'I can't say if it was deliberate or accidental but we have had very hot weather recently, approaching thirty degrees centigrade a few times so, for example, if the remains were left out in that for a few days and then say, submerged in water for a few days, or vice versa, that might well result in the skeletal condition we found'.

'Maybe when they killed her, they threw her in a river or lake or even the sea, then a few days later, they were afraid she'd be found or something and moved her?' suggested Hennessy.

'That's your side of the investigation but I'm hoping the tests they're running now will provide us with a better insight, including in relation to saturation in water, type of water, et cetera. The pieces of clothing might be particularly relevant in that regard, cloth – depending on the material used – doesn't deteriorate at the same rate as bones, skin, muscle, et cetera'.

Hennessy was taking notes and running several different scenarios in his head as he listened to the Chief State Pathologist.

'Getting back to the place we found her, might that be one of several?' asked Hennessy after a pause, 'In other words, did they cut her up and spread the parts in different places?'

'No, we recovered virtually all of her bones on the site, plus an examination of the edges doesn't show any signs that a cutting tool like a knife or chainsaw was used. The construction equipment would have been sufficient to break up rather than mutilate the corpse' replied Lubenski.

'Okay, we need to find the murder site' sighed Hennessy, more to himself than to his colleague, as his phone alerted him to an incoming call from AJ.

'I have to take another call Oskar but one quick question please; you mentioned bone marrow, does that mean we were able to extract DNA?' quizzed Hennessy.

'Correct, when we have the full profile, we'll check it against all the DNA databases and missing person reports'.

'Great stuff, thanks Oskar' said an enthusiastic Hennessy as he ended that call and took the new one.

'Gar, our new team member's just been stabbed'.

Chapter 17

It was difficult for Fran Balfe to decide if the car parked across the road from *Village Antiques* was waiting for someone to come out of the nearby pub or if the two occupants were casing his shop but either way, it made him nervous. He didn't know how long it was there for but he had first noticed it around an hour ago and it was now almost half ten on a dark, cloudy night. The car itself was quite nondescript, silver with four doors and quite dirty looking. He couldn't make out the registration from his observation point at the front door of his unlit shop and he wasn't sufficiently familiar with or interested in motor vehicles to discern its make.

It was also possible he reflected as he stepped back from the door that he was becoming a little bit paranoid. His wife Rebecca was now gone for over six weeks on a buying mission and he had heard nothing from her, despite regularly berating her previously for not keeping in touch. Their business bank account showed no transactions by her for weeks although he knew that she preferred to use her own credit card for hotel charges and he had no access to that account. It wasn't unusual that there was no activity on her mobile phone when he examined the bill that came in as she tended to use hotel or restaurant landlines on the rare occasions that she did make contact. He had attempted to track her down – using her maiden and married names - by ringing the central reservations offices of the hotel chains that she favoured but that proved time-consuming and unsuccessful. The default mantra used by customer service staff in every organisation in Europe nowadays, as far as he could tell, was 'GDPR', general data protection regulation, the EU-inspired privacy law that came into force in 2018. That was also quoted to him when he contacted the Dublin Airport Authority – in a case more of desperation than hope he had to admit – to request that they check their cameras for the date Rebecca left with a view to establishing what flight she got on. Asking them to check if her car was still parked in one of the many airport car parks was equally fruitless; he wasn't even sure how finding her car would help to find her. He also knew from prior experience that contacting airlines to request flight information was pointless, even if he did have a reservation number, which he didn't have on this occasion. If she had succumbed to an illness or been involved in an accident, the medical or police authorities in that country would surely have been in touch, he would tell himself on these occasions.

It wasn't just him though who went uncontacted, none of Rebecca's family or friends heard from her during these buying trips either. Not that that was any consolation.

He sat down on a plastic chair they used for dusting higher shelves and contemplated his predicament. His wife was missing, was that the correct term to use? She was certainly uncontactable as far as he was concerned. No matter how many times in the past they discussed and argued about it, nothing changed. He sat around the shop wondering and worrying about where she was and when she'd be back whilst she travelled the planet to engage in her almost obsessive pursuit of rare and valuable antiques that could be picked up for a bargain. Then she would arrive back unannounced and behave as if she had just gone to the local shop for milk. Not any longer he decided there and then, he was going to put his foot down. It didn't matter how many times she defended her travels by claiming that she did it for the business, for *their* business, he was determined to demand phone contact at least once a week in future, business or no business. That was something else that was bothering him over the past few weeks. Sales were virtually non-existent. Even allowing for Covid restrictions, no viewing appointments were being made and the level of activity on their website was dwindling to an all-time low. Maybe that was what he needed to do, redesign the website to make it more attractive. That, and invest in some advertising to increase interest. But redesigning websites and online advertising entailed money, and that was a commodity that was in short supply.

After a few minutes, Fran carefully looked out the front door again. The car was gone.

Or maybe I'm just lonely without Rebecca he told himself as he took out his mobile phone to ring the Gardaí and report a missing person.

Chapter 18

Probably the first thing that alerted Detective Garda Johnny Lennon to something suspicious about the woman walking down the main aisle of the Shamrock Bar in a blue and white striped staff uniform was the tray of glasses she was carrying. It was shaking. Not violently, more like a tremor. Creating a chime but not a particularly melodious one. It also struck him that the woman was walking away from the bar counter yet the glasses were dirty. She fitted the description so he motioned to his Garda colleague that he was approaching her.

Probably the next thing that he should have seen as she put the tray down on a table was the dining knife in her right hand when she spun around and plunged it in to his left side. He felt a sharp jab in the ribs and reached out to grab her arm as he fell to the ground. Pain and a leaking sound was promptly followed by a skirmish taking place above him.

The female Garda accompanying Lennon had already disarmed the deportee, wrestled her to the ground, and had started handcuffing her when AJ reached the scene. She could see the blood and hear from the gasping that he was in trouble so adjusted his position and told him he'd be fine before calling Airport Police Control and summoning the ambulance that was based in the fire station. She knew that would be a faster option than waiting for a unit from Beaumont hospital about eight kilometres away. Looking at the wound and the bloodied knife on the floor she figured that considerable force must have been applied. The male Garda that she blamed for this debacle reached her as she was pressing her handkerchief against the injury. Customers and staff had gathered around to watch the spectacle.

'Get them back and get me more dressing' AJ demanded, glaring at the embarrassed man.

The two Airport Police officers who had been assisting with the search heard the broadcast from Control and arrived on the scene just as the deportee made a desperate effort to get out from under the female Garda. Such was her strength she almost succeeded.

'Can you call a car and get her out of here?' asked AJ of the Airport Police.

Lennon's breathing seemed to be getting more laboured and AJ tried to readjust his position to give him some relief whilst re-assuring him that the ambulance was on its way. The more force she applied to the wound the more he moaned in pain and she was pretty sure that meant at least one rib was broken. She gazed again at the handcuffed woman being lifted off the floor and moved away from the area. The noise from the ambulance siren was music to her ears and she let Lennon know that he'd be in Beaumont in no time. Carrying a bunch of serviettes from the bar counter the male Garda returned and kneeled down to help, his right knee immediately soaked in blood.

'Go with her' AJ instructed, motioning to the deportee being led away, 'she's your responsibility'.

Turning back to her colleague, she tried to comfort him again. 'Take shallow breaths Johnny, you're doing fine'.

The stretcher crew went to work as soon as they got there and AJ let them do their job, standing up and asking the Airport Police to cordon off the tables around them as a crime scene. Within two minutes, there was an oxygen mask and IV on Lennon and he was being wheeled away at pace.

AJ held her phone with shaking, blood-stained hands as she gave Hennessy the bad news.

Chapter 19

The express Red long term car park lies just over a kilometre from the passenger terminals at Dublin Airport. It has a land area of some fifteen acres, a capacity of eight thousand spaces, and a 24-hour shuttle service operating approximately every ten minutes during busy periods. Surface water from the car park drains into the Cuckoo Stream, which commences at Dublin Airport, flows under the M1 motorway at Toberbunny, and connects to the Mayne River close to Wellfield Bridge.

Such details were of no concern to Cormac Tierney as he drove his fifteen-year-old Mercedes E200 around the car park just after eleven o'clock in the morning. His only interest was finding a suitable place to relieve himself. He knew there were toilets at the exit but he was in the furthest zone away from it and the pressure from too many drinks with work mates the night before was telling. Truth be told, he probably shouldn't have been driving at all. There was also the matter of time. His flight to New York was scheduled to depart at one o'clock and he still had to navigate through airport security screening, airline security screening, and U.S Immigration. He could see a shuttle bus cruising around the outer ring road of the zone but he wasn't sure if he had missed it. Finding an empty space was proving much more difficult than he had expected and, so far, any that he had come across were either directly overlooked by the M50 airport exit at the end of the car park or by the aforementioned shuttle bus ring road.

After ten minutes of searching, he decided in frustration to park in the next available space and then look for a sheltered spot to spend a penny. His preference was to reverse into spaces but time was of the essence on this occasion, flight-wise and bladder-wise. He locked the car with the key fob as he trotted towards the perimeter whilst scanning the area for a concealed location, knowing that his irregular gait was betraying his urgent mission. Seconds turned into minutes and as he was on the point of returning to his car and driving like a maniac to the exit toilets, he noticed a dip in the terrain beyond the boundary fence between the edge of the car park and the M1 motorway. There appeared to be plenty of small trees and large bushes around the dip but, infuriatingly, he couldn't see any gaps in the fence. He estimated its height at two and a half metres when he reached it and the barbed wire on the top ruled out any intentions of trying to climb over it. Not to mention how it would look if anyone saw him. Cursing himself for not driving straight to the exit toilets on entering the car park, he was resigned to wetting himself when he spotted loose cabling at the bottom of the fence beside a metal pillar about twenty metres away. Crab-like he ran to it and stretched the wire just wide enough to scramble through.

Have I just aided and abetted car thieves by enhancing their entry point he was asking himself as he hurriedly descended the dip, only to be halted abruptly by the sight of a steam flowing through it. In all my years using this car park I never knew this was here he said to himself whilst thanking the heavens for its existence as the hedgerow it nurtured provided perfect cover for him to conduct his business.

Smiling broadly from the relief he was experiencing beside the bank of the stream he had time to take in his unfrequented surroundings. Except that they may not have been as unfrequented as he thought he surmised when he focussed on a stretch of grass a few metres away that appeared to have been recently trampled on. It seemed to have damp stains also even though there hadn't been any rain for several weeks. He was convinced that it had been lain on but unsure by what or by whom. The possibility of some type of animal or animals came to mind. Or possibly a secretive courting couple? But the longer he took in and thought about the scene, the more something about it made him feel uneasy. The stream was virtually silent but the traffic noise from the nearby motorway was clearly audible. Perhaps it was the dichotomy between this oasis of seclusion set between a busy car park on one side and the hustle and bustle of the Dublin – Belfast motorway on the other that spooked him a little bit. Or perhaps it was the anxiety he was already feeling about catching his flight combined with the after-effects of his alcohol consumption the previous evening that made him extra edgy and extra brave but something didn't feel right.

He was ready to leave now but felt he had to investigate the clearing further before dismissing it as nothing to be concerned with so he slowly ventured over.

That's when he saw a set of broken reading glasses with red marks and pieces of metal and glass that looked like they came from a mobile phone. And that's when he saw that the damp stains were the colour of blood.

Chapter 20

'Was there any difficulty?'

'Some persuasion needed'.

'You got it, that's the important thing' said fine art and antiquities dealer Norman Prendergast as he opened a cardboard box that one of two men standing in front of him had just handed over.

The three men were meeting in the dimly lit storeroom at the back of Prendergast's shop. It was almost two in the morning and Prendergast knew that few people would be around the area and more importantly, that there were no CCTV cameras in the vicinity of the rear entrance. One of the two naked bulbs hanging on long cables from the galvanised roof was switched on but it contained a twenty-five watt bulb that made a feeble effort to shed any illumination on proceedings. The floor was concrete and the walls brick with heavy duty shelving on two sides and large wooden crates scattered around the room. He opened the wrapping paper inside the box and took a small torch from his coat pocket to inspect the merchandise. His eyes beamed with satisfaction and his smile radiated approval. When he was finished his examination he turned off the torch and turned to the two men.

'Mission successfully completed, your payment is on that coffee table' he said pointing to an unsteady looking wooden structure that could easily have been mistaken for a bench. There was a stack of books on one side and a large white envelope in the middle. One of the men took an equally unstable chair and sat down at the table to count the envelope's contents.

Prendergast watched nervously as the man slowly removed the elastic bands and laid the currency out in neat bundles. It wasn't that Prendergast was worried that it was short, he had checked it himself twice. He was tense because he found the company of these two men to be anything but pleasurable. In fact, he found their presence distasteful. He didn't even know their names nor any details about their backgrounds. This was a good thing in his opinion, the less he knew the better. He had learned about their services during the pandemic when he was having no success securing payment from a purchaser on a handmade, natural green, jade necklace. When he described his frustration to a pal over a drink in his favourite watering hole across the river from his shop in Smithfield square, his pal assured him that there were two men who guaranteed satisfaction in such matters. Two days later, a small package was pushed in to his letter box and inside it was a very basic mobile phone with a charger. He turned it on and a few hours later received a call setting out the men's terms and conditions. All they needed to know was the amount to be recovered and the name and address of the person that it was to be recovered from. Within twenty four hours he answered another call confirming that the debt had been paid and requesting details on the handover. That evening he got his money and they got theirs. He was no expert in accents but if he was pushed, he would say the one he communicated with was Scandinavian. The other one he had no idea. Their meetings were always during darkness hours and in unlit rooms so he couldn't even accurately describe them or the difference between them. All he could say, reluctantly, was that they were both of medium height and build, with fair hair. Not that he would ever dare to provide their description to anyone. He knew better. That was what spoked him. When he heard detailed reports of their methods, often from TV news. Their propensity to resort almost instantaneously to extreme violence regularly garnered headlines. The comment from his pal that had put him in touch with them also served to keep him alert: "*keep your distance and never, ever cross them*".

'Where are we at on the dealer in Killiney?'

'Watching him but so far all he does is walk around his shop in the dark. He hasn't moved. Is it that you would like for us to be more proactive?' said one of the men.

'No, just keep watching him'.

The less these men knew about Prendergast's business the better he liked it. Mind you, he was thinking as the seated man finished counting, they never asked him about it anyway. Which was a good thing, as he had darker plans for the art dealer.

Chapter 21

'Hundred percent Detective Inspector'.

'And what exactly is 'pneumothorax'?'

'It's when air gets out of a punctured lung and gathers between the lung and the chest wall Detective Inspectors, at least that's what I understand from the doctors' answered Detective Johnny Lennon from his hospital bed.

Visiting his newest team member in St. Anne's ward at Beaumont Hospital, situated roughly midway between the airport and the city centre, was not where Hennessy had seen himself as part of this murder investigation yet this was where himself and AJ had arrived on a wet but warm July morning. There were six beds in the room and Lennon's was beside the window on the left. The curtains were pulled around the bed and nurses moved between the patients checking on various things. There was an IV in Lennon's left arm and he looked a little uncomfortable.

'So it's not gonna kill you?' said AJ trying to lighten the mood.

'No' smiled Lennon back at her, 'a collapsed lung is not life-threatening. They put a tube in between the ribs with a pump attached and sucked the air out'.

'Sounds painful' said Hennessy.

'Looks worse than it feels. The pain comes from breathing too goddam hard' answered Lennon. 'Or laughing' he continued, looking at AJ.

'Seemed like you lost a lot of blood?' queried AJ.

'Not enough to need a transfusion. They did a chest x-ray and said there was no other damage, thankfully' responded Lennon.

'You did well to spot her Johnny; wasn't that obvious from the photo we had' said AJ.

'She had dirty glasses on the tray and was walking away from the counter plus I noticed a slight tremble in her hands carrying the tray. Then she dropped her gaze when I got closer to her' explained Lennon.

'It was good work, she was dangerous' said Hennessy.

'Would have been better if I'd seen the goddam knife, feckin' bitch. Anyway, you got her'.

'Guy in charge of deporting her won't be doing that job much longer. Last I heard, she'll be deported rather than kept here and charged with assaulting a Garda. The Bulgarians have more serious charges waiting for her' said AJ.

A nurse appeared at Lennon's bedside and quietly and efficiently changed his IV, gave him two tablets with some water, and updated his chart.

'So what happens next?' queried Hennessy as his phone started to ring.

'They wait for the lung to re-inflate. They're saying six or seven weeks out of action but no way do I need that long' responded Lennon.

Hennessy was backing out of the curtains and answering his phone as Lennon finished his sentence so he turned to AJ.

'What a fucking first day as a murder squad detective huh?'

'No one says 'murder squad' any more Johnny plus I'd put it down as a great first day: you caught a killer and got stabbed. A lot more eventful than my first day; I was given a shitload of files and told to record them in a musty old ledger, complete waste of time' replied AJ in a cheerful tone.

'Yeah I suppose' muttered Lennon, 'better than romance fraud anyway. Telling some poor aul one or aul fella in their seventies that the twenty-year-old they gave thirty grand to doesn't exist. Poor fuckers are always devastated, goddam heart-breaking to see'.

'Wait till you're informing some parent in their seventies that their daughter or son was killed. They never get over it' said AJ.

They could hear Hennessy talking beside the window outside the curtains but couldn't hear what he was saying.

'So what's the story with this investigation AJ: why so few detectives on it? Is it going anywhere? Is Hennessy on top of it?' asked Lennon.

'Of course he's on top of it, we're making progress but we need to do more digging. Resources are tight with all the gang stuff but we're sure to get more help soon, especially now that you're out of action' responded AJ.

'That's what I was trying to say to Hennessy; I don't have to be out for six weeks, I could easily help with desk research when I get out of here in a few days. I could do the 'digging' at home?' pleaded Lennon.

'Hennessy would have to approve it and you'd have to be officially passed fit to return to light duties for that Johnny, and neither is unlikely. Play the hero when you get the chance, you caught a killer!'

'I did in me arse AJ. I saw someone who fitted the photo and approached her, got knifed, hit the floor like a stone, and ended up here....hardly a goddam Marvel film hero! I didn't even disarm the bitch and we don't know for certain that she killed anyone' fumed Lennon.

'Thought that was where the eagle tattoo came from: king of the skies, eagle-eyed, strong, all that shit?' queried AJ with a smile on her face.

'When did you see that?' asked Lennon pushing his pyjama sleeve back. 'That was a joke when I won a clay pigeon shooting competition on a weekend away with the lads...too many pints, blah, blah, blah' explained Lennon.

The phone call that Hennessy was on seemed to be coming to an end.

'If you're that enthusiastic to help Johnny, we could really do with someone checking the background of all the people we've interviewed so far, see if they have any criminal records or connections, you know the drill, but you need to convince Gar first' suggested AJ.

Lennon was smiling when Hennessy stuck his head around the curtain but didn't get to make his request.

'That was Campbell from the Technical Office, they think they've found the murder scene'.

Chapter 22

Having a copy of his wife's passport and a recent photo at a birthday dinner made Fran Balfe's task of describing her when he visited Dun Laoghaire Garda Station a lot easier. He felt he was being taken seriously when he told the young Garda on desk duty how long it had been since he last saw Rebecca but when he admitted that she regularly embarked on overseas buying trips without making contact, his credibility seemed to fade somewhat. At least that was his impression. Not having any previous experience of dealing with the Gardaí made him a long way short of being an expert when it came to such matters. Nor was his wife. But that should be a good thing shouldn't it, he was reflecting on, as the young Garda continued to ask questions. Maybe they were trained to be disbelieving in their approach to the filing of missing person reports?

Although she looked sympathetic at times; there was also an air of suspicion in her demeanour, Balfe felt.

There again, the hesitancy with which he had walked through the double doors of the public office donning a dark red face mask may well have contributed to any scepticism on the part of the officer. It wasn't Balfe's first time to enter the station; he had visited numerous times to pick up Driving Licence application forms, get Passport Applications stamped, and even once to show his car insurance disc when he was stopped one evening at a Garda checkpoint and the disc on display was out of date. The Garda he dealt with that night was also dubious Balfe now recalled, even when he had explained to him that he had a valid, current insurance disc but had simply neglected to swap it out with the old one in the plastic windscreen display. Those previous visits he deemed 'housekeeping' in nature. Today's was a much more serious matter.

The public office was clean and brightly lit when Balfe entered. On the left hand side there were three plastic hatches along a wooden counter, two of them closed and shuttered. To the right of the counter, a large brown display stand contained a wide range of application forms and explanation leaflets. Then there was a door that led into the back office and to the right of that again, a noticeboard with warnings about Covid procedures, upcoming road closures, and littering fines. The walls were beige and had very few marks or scraps. A small black camera at the back of the room kept an eye on proceedings and probably accounted for the absence of any graffiti or scratched curse words, Balfe figured.

There were two members of the public in front of him. One middle-aged woman getting served at the counter, and the second a tall, slim, young man with a crew cut wearing dirty turquoise tracksuit bottoms and a navy hoodie. Both customers wore face masks and were adhering to the clearly-marked yellow social distancing stickers on the grey linoleum floor. Balfe kept his head down with his folder of papers under his arm while he waited. The middle-aged woman appeared to be querying a dog licence or a dog warden's fine or something to do with her dog, as far as he could overhear. He was glad that the dog wasn't with her. She became a little agitated but never rude as the conversation with the Garda on the counter continued and eventually folded up the piece of paper she was pointing to, put it in her handbag, and left. When the next customer in line approached the counter, the officer told him she would be back in a few minutes and promptly pulled down the shutter. The young man ushered a highly derogatory expletive but in a hushed tone. He turned to look at Balfe but Balfe's long-standing policy of not making eye contact with anyone who posed a threat to his personal safety had already been successfully deployed.

Fortunately – from Balfe's point of view - the Garda returned as promised, briefly listened to the customer, picked up a ledger with a pen attached by string, and slid it across the counter. The young man signed it, said nothing, and walked out. Fran could hear somebody else coming in at the same time but he was focussed on the first statement he would make to the Garda. He had been practicing it for long enough at this stage.

'Hi, my name is Fran Balfe. I own and live in the antiques shop in Killiney, as does my wife Rebecca. I'd like to report my wife as missing'.

After the initial series of questions at the counter, some of which Balfe answered confidently and coherently and more of which he struggled nervously with, the officer asked to be excused for a few minutes and pulled down the shutter again. Balfe could now hear sighs from at least two people behind him but dared not turn around. He hoped firstly that they didn't know him, and secondly that they didn't listen in on his mask-distorted mutterings that were intended to be clear, precise answers.

Minutes passed but before the shutter was raised, the door on his right opened and a different Garda – this time a slightly older man in blue jeans and a black 'Thin Lizzy' sweatshirt - approached him and asked if he would follow him inside. When he sat down at the side of a very untidy desk, the officer introduced himself as Stephen and explained that there would be more privacy here to complete the report.

There were five or six other desks scattered around this large room and several plain clothes and uniformed Gardaí busily talking on the phone or typing at a computer or searching through a filing cabinet. The lighting was bright and the walls were a clean if bland beige colour. Balfe's presence went entirely unnoticed to them, which pleased him a lot. Stephen proceeded to repeat many of the questions already asked but seemed to Balfe to be writing down more comprehensive versions of the replies. Balfe couldn't quite make out whether this was the old form or a new one. The pattern of the interview took on the same semblance as the one with the Garda on the public counter. Initially, Stephen didn't strike him as betraying any specific judgement – good or bad - as far as his attitude was concerned. He was asking questions in a neutral tone and then recording the responses. But as time and questions went on, the Garda's tone and body language – at least in Balfe's eyes – became increasingly nuanced, to the point of disbelief in one or two instances.

To be fair to the officer, Balfe's level of discomfort followed more or less the same path. The questions about age, occupation, health, siblings, history of travel, medication, and relationships with neighbours and business acquaintances were quite straightforward to answer but when it got to discussing his marriage, frequency and severity of arguments ('every marriage has them' the officer reassured him with a fake smile), any financial problems, enemies, illnesses, and any recent changes in behaviour, Balfe became distinctly unsettled. He kept telling himself to calm down, that he had nothing to hide, but that was easier said than done when you're sitting in a police station. The walls almost imposed an assumption of guilt.

After about fifteen minutes, the officer paused, flicked through the pages of notes in front of him, pulled his chair closer to Balfe, and leaned in to him. 'Can I be candid with you Mr. Balfe?' posed the officer.

Taken aback Balfe nodded in the affirmative.

'What *exactly* is motivating you to make this report?'

Balfe looked bemused.

'No history of illness, no known enemies, a long sales trip with no contact which had happened previously, an antique that your wife didn't want stored in the safe, and possibly a suspicious car parked across the road observing your shop a few times, *possibly*. Did I miss something?' queried Stephen.

'No, well nothing specific but why isn't that sufficient? I know my wife officer, something has happened!' stormed Balfe in frustration.

'Let me be more clear Mr. Balfe, if I may. No threat has been made against your wife, she has no enemies that you know of, she wasn't carrying a large amount of cash as far as you are aware, nobody has tried to break into your shop...and your wife has a history of not maintaining contact. I don't see any indication that she might be in danger here' Stephen pointed out, before taking a deep breath and continuing, 'unless of course...'

'Unless what?' snapped Fran.

Stephen stared down at the paperwork in front of him, slowly breathed out, and then turned sharply to Balfe.

'Mr. Balfe, did your wife come to any harm at your hands?'

Chapter 23

Senior Technical Officer Aoife Campbell was standing just inside the crime scene tape when Hennessy and AJ arrived at the back of the red, long-term car park at Dublin Airport. A white tent covered part of the site cordoned off with the yellow tape. The Cuckoo stream meandered by oblivious to the serious goings on. Sunshine intermittently broke through the stubborn clouds after earlier rain. There were two marked Garda patrol cars parked beside the large white Technical van. The location of the Garda activity allowed for normal car park operations to continue with minimum inconvenience but both private vehicles and transfer buses slowed down as they drove past, their passengers eager to ascertain what was happening.

'Least we won't need the Water Unit!' said an enthusiastic Campbell as she approached the two detectives.

The two detectives looked puzzled.

'The stream...it's shallow so our people can search it' explained Campbell.

Neither officer appeared impressed.

'It's definitely blood and there's definitely a lot of it but whether it's your victim's blood we don't know yet. Your people are searching along the banks of the stream and they've already taken a statement from the guy who rang it in; he was rushing for a flight' she continued.

The conversation was noisily interrupted by an aircraft with red and blue livery flying directly overhead as it landed on the southern runway. It was low enough to read the airline name and to see the fully-engaged landing gear. The sound of vehicle traffic from the nearby motorway was a whisper by comparison.

'What else did you find?' asked Hennessy when the noise dissipated.

'A broken pair of reading glasses and small metal bits that I'm pretty certain are from a mobile' answered Campbell.

'Is there a sim or internal memory card in the phone parts?' probed AJ quickly.

'Not that I could see, no' replied Campbell.

'What about the reading glasses, might they be prescribed?' queried Hennessy who now recognised a Sergeant from Santry station amongst the uniformed officers huddled around the stream-side of the tent.

'We'll follow that up but the glass is pretty shattered; we're still collecting pieces of it. The frame is badly mangled but we'll check for any markings that would allow us to identify the maker or owner when we get everything back to the lab. And of course we'll conduct fingerprint tests' answered Campbell.

'Is there anyway of telling how long all this has been here?' asked AJ.

'We should be able to date the blood fairly accurately, yes. We use a technique called Raman spectroscopy by shining a laser on a blood sample and then measuring the intensity of scattered light. Using advanced statistics on the results, it's fairly accurate provided the blood stain is less than two years old. It's actually a wonderful piece of science and it's non-destructive; the process doesn't destroy the sample so you can repeat it or run other tests, like DNA sequencing' responded an over-enthusiastic Campbell.

'So why didn't we use that with the blood from the construction site?' probed AJ.

'Well, the age of the blood stain isn't necessarily the time of death of the victim and pathologists are mainly interested in the latter. A victim could have their own blood stains on their clothes or body that are completely unrelated to their time of death. I did speak to Dr. Lubenski about it given the circumstances the remains were found in but he felt that the blood was too badly degraded from soil and diluted with water to give an accurate deposition reading. He figured the insect expert he knew could analyse the bones and their bug residents to provide a fairly accurate time of death' explained Campbell.

'But he concluded that the volume of blood at that site was less than he would expect if it was the murder scene?' asked Hennessy.

Another aircraft – this time louder, bigger and noisier – stopped Campbell from providing an answer for over forty seconds.

'Absolutely. And from what I've seen here, we're dealing with a substantial volume of blood.

Fortunately we've had fairly dry weather for the past few weeks so the samples we've taken look good quality and should allow us to give you a good estimate of volume'.

Hennessy and AJ were still mulling over the information when Campbell continued.

'I can still run RS tests on the blood from the runway site if you wish; we would normally do it anyway as part of our protocols but things are so backed up at the moment, we're way behind on finalising reports' suggested Campbell.

'If this is our victim's murder site, both dates – the bug guy's from the bugs and yours from the blood - should be more or less the same, right?' asked AJ, trying to understand the science herself.

'Corroboratory, yes...more or less' confirmed Campbell.

Hennessy was staring at the Cuckoo stream a few metres away as he recalled the point made by Lubenski that the advanced stage of decomposition the remains were found in could have come about from humid weather and / or being submerged in water.

AJ meanwhile was considering the unpleasant possibility that this was the murder scene of some other poor unfortunate or, even worse, that the high volume of blood found was spilled from more than one individual.

Both detectives were awoken from their musings by the sudden appearance of the Sergeant from Santry beside them. He described the tasks he had assigned to his officers and asked Hennessy if there was anything else he wanted done.

'Not at this stage thanks. Searching the banks and the stream itself is sufficient. We're lucky that it's a fairly small, constrained site. Make sure it's guarded tonight and I'll be in touch tomorrow; we should know more when the lab results come in'.

Hennessy turned almost instinctively to AJ as she usually had something else to ask for, usually something he hadn't thought of or, he liked to think, something he hadn't yet thought of. AJ's thoughts however were elsewhere. She was gazing almost straight up – left palm shading her eyes from the peeping sunshine - at a twenty metre high lighting mast on the other side of the white tent. Hennessy was about to ask her what caught her attention when he saw it himself.

The CCTV camera at the top of the mast.

Chapter 24

'Unfortunate? I would be less euphemistic in my terminology Garoid. You have been shot, Detective Jenkinson has been shot at, and now your newest team member – on his first day mind – lies in a hospital bed with a knife injury. That's more than fucking unfortunate, that's unprecedented in this department' stated DS Marie Brophy.

'Nevertheless ma'am, I do believe we are making progress on the case. We may well have found the murder scene and we have a good idea of the time of death so that should enable us to -'.

'That's not actually why I called you in Garoid' interrupted Brophy, 'I'm sure you are making progress but I need to inform you about changes in your reporting relationship'.

Hennessy sat back in his chair at the table in Brophy's office and took a deep breath. It was unusual for Brophy to call you into her office for an update when she was under pressure to solve the feuding gangs' cases and get some of their leaders off the streets. He had feared that Brophy would be disappointed with his work on the case and may have decided he wasn't up to it, either because it was too soon after returning to duty or because it was beyond his competence level. If he was correct, he hoped against hope that it was the former reason. To be taken off a case or have another detective helicoptered in to take it over would be a career blow that he could ill afford at this stage in his. It wouldn't say that or anything like it on his personnel file of course but the reputational damage from getting removed or replaced when in charge of a homicide investigation – even on a low-profile one - was akin to sporting a hat with '*screwed up, not to be trusted*' emblazoned on it. Everyone on the force knew that. Nor would the brownie points that he picked up from getting seriously wounded in the line of duty save him. You're only as good as your last case, end of.

'The thing is' explained Brophy, taking a deep breath herself, 'the gods – for their own atavistic purposes no doubt - have seen fit to afflict me with a malady that will require the relinquishment of my current duties'.

The frown on Hennessy's face showed concern but he couldn't deny that he was also feeling a certain amount of relief.

'I'm very sorry to hear that ma'am, I hope the illness isn't serious?'

'Cancer Garoid, and not a particularly pulchritudinous one...but I'm reasonably fit and my medical people are highly qualified so....' replied a hesitant Brophy.

Hennessy had never seen his boss show any sign of weakness or vulnerability and wanted to show his support without coming across as insincere. Her office had always appeared neat and organised to him but then most of the time he felt on the defensive when he visited it so evaluating the decor was not high on his priorities. Now, the lack of family photos, colourful pictures or bright colours gave it an austere look in his opinion, even bleak. Most offices in the older buildings at Garda HQ in Dublin's Phoenix Park had similar colour schemes – beige walls with grey linoleum floors – but their occupants invariably attempted to personalise them, often with small furnishings from their homes. He recalled one senior officer who bought dark red paint and spent several evenings applying it, only to be informed by one of his superiors shortly afterwards that the Office of Public Works was responsible for maintaining the offices and such refurbishments required their prior approval.

'I'm sure you'll be back in no time ma'am, you're badly needed around here' said Hennessy in an encouraging tone.

'Thank you Detective but I've been long enough around this organisation to understand that my sickness and subsequent absence will be forgotten in a glancingly swift manner. The world keeps turning, criminals continue committing crimes, the perfidious fucks, we lock some up, more take their place...and so on' said Brophy.

'You've made a huge contribution to the force ma'am, a lot of those criminals are locked up because of you' said Hennessy, deciding as he spoke that he was now appearing disingenuous and it was time to shut up.

Now much was known in the Garda circles Hennessy frequented about Brophy's private life, which was how she wanted it apparently. There were rumours of course. There were always rumours. The less that was known, the more rumours there were. She was going through a divorce, had no children, loved playing golf, and was on the verge of retiring; that was pretty much the summation of the rumours.

'Again, thank you for your kind sentiments but the more immediate issue is that I'm not going to be around here for quite a while, if ever, so I wanted to tell you that face-to-face and to inform you about who was taking over...at least I was until an hour or so again but it now transpires that the changes that were due to be announced later this afternoon have been put on hold. Why, I know not. Just when one believes one knows everything that's going on, one discovers that some unknown fuckwit actually knows a lot more, most unedifying. Be that as it may, I'm still glad I got to tell you in person that I'm not going to be in charge. These things are important I believe'.

Brophy's frame was always somewhat slight, in stark contrast to her fearsome reputation as a stickler for high standards and hard work. The testimonies she provided in high profile criminal cases were often used for training purposes at the Garda College in Tullamore and whilst she could be hard on those who reported to her, she was also considered fair and supportive. Now, she seemed to Hennessy to be a little greyer, less feisty and focussed but there again she had a lot on her mind and could well be on medication, he surmised.

'I appreciate that ma'am. If you don't mind my asking, how soon do you leave?'

'Let me put it to you this way Detective; in less than forty-eight hours time, I am due on an operating table in St. Vincent's Hospital to have most of my stomach removed'.

Chapter 25

The jog along Clontarf promenade as the sun was setting had become a highlight in AJ's day. She enjoyed it even more since she moved to the area, and going home to mechanic partner Ray always gave her a warm feeling, no matter how tired she was. Running proved both physically and mentally healthy for her, particularly since the Covid-19 pandemic struck. Her now deceased parents both embraced outdoor exercise, her dad jogging and her mother swimming. She remembered when she was growing up that they both also loved long walks, extolling the virtues of exercise on a regular basis. AJ figured that was probably why she took up jogging, although she didn't exactly take to it like a duck to water. Heading out on cold, wet evenings never appealed to her and, if she did summon up sufficient courage to do it, she kept those runs short. More often than not back then, she put it off for another day. The older she got however, the more she saw the benefits of pulling on her gear, setting her fitness app, putting her earphones in, pressing shuffle on her music playlist that she titled *Fun run*, and jogging for anything from 10 km to 15 km, depending on her mood. Food for the soul she called it when friends and colleagues asked about her interest in it.

Approaching the newly renovated Clontarf Baths this evening, AJ found herself thinking back to those early days of exercising, and to her parents. She figured they'd be proud of her keeping it up, and even extending her distances. Not that distance and personal bests were the reasons her parents exercised, they simply appreciated having the health to be able to do it. Until they didn't have the health to do it of course. But that brought negative thoughts to AJ and she was determined not to be melancholic on her runs. Her father used to tell her to smile as she ran after he heard someone comment sarcastically that 'joggers never smile'. Taylor Swift's *You belong with Me* was playing as she deliberately turned her thoughts to things that were going well in her life. Ray came to mind first. Since they moved in together, they had been getting on really well. He was personable, supportive and funny. They often called over to his parents in Castleknock and she could see where he got his personality; his mother in particular had exactly the same sense of humour and fun. By trade he was a mechanic but he loved the technology components in cars and much preferred working on electric vehicles that ones with combustion engines.

Taylor Swift had given way to her musical collaborator Ed Sheeran by the time AJ reached the wooden bridge that leads to Bull Island and North Bull Wall. She loved the fact that the single-lane bridge dated back over two hundred years and she loved the sound of the creaking that the wooden beams made as you passed over. That brought her to her career. How many conversations had Ray and she engaged in about life in the Garda Siochana? From a promising start to a controversial firearm discharging incident, to a demotion, to signs that the higher ups might be forgiving her, it was all so complicated and confusing. Two interlocking thoughts consistently came to the fore: did she want to stay in the force and, did the force want her to stay? Therein lay the dilemma: was she being involved in serious investigations because they valued her ability or because they were desperate? If she considered it the former, maybe she could still forge a rewarding career in the guards, but if it was the latter, should she get out now? And who could tell her which it was?

Having passed the Royal Dublin Golf Club, AJ was now on Dollymount Strand and listening to Weeknd's *Save your Tears* when she deliberately adjusted her thinking to a current, positive aspect of her career: her official assignment to a homicide inquiry. Whatever the reasoning behind her appointment, she was going to make the most of it. Her relationship with Hennessy had a lot of baggage but he was singularly focussed – as far as she could tell – on getting it resolved. That gave them common purpose. The investigation so far had been fully in keeping with the approach that they were both trained in. More resources could always be used but that was out of her hands. Some of the interviews, for example, were being conducted by a sole detective and, whilst that wasn't against protocol, it certainly wasn't ideal. The preferred standard is for two investigators to participate in interviews; this provided more balance, more control, and more insights. In addition, cross-analysis – identifying connections, consistencies and contradictions across the people spoken to and the information collected – should be undertaken as they went but they didn't have the people, particularly now that Lennon was out of the picture. Maybe Brophy would allocate someone else when Hennessy met her?

She could see the lighthouse on Howth Head so clearly tonight. And the sprinkling of pleasure boats and yachts enjoying the warm evening. Dog-walkers were availing of the nice weather also and there were even a few swimmers in the water. The sand was pretty churned up after the day's activities but AJ knew the route well enough to hug the sand dunes, where there was more grip. Her fitness app beeped and informed her that 7 km had been achieved so far, that and her time per kilometre, her running cadence, and her expected finishing time. Only the first piece of information was of interest to her as she kept on moving and thinking, and smiling.

The big break they needed of course was to identify the victim; that would instantly unlock a plethora of new inquiry avenues. AJ knew that, and Hennessy knew that. Heck even knifing-victim Lennon probably knew that she concluded as she turned at the first exit road and re-traced the same route back, this time with a good view of the cargo ships sailing in and out of Dublin Port. Forensics was key whatever way you looked at it: establishing the murder scene, approximate time of death, definitively stating the cause of death, embellishing the profile of the victim, and hopefully, getting a DNA match from their databases. Then there was technology: narrowing down the time of death and enhancing the profile of the victim to estimate features such as height and weight, would afford the investigation considerably more focus in their trawl of CCTV systems both at the airport and in the surrounding areas. Specifically, if the crime scene reported in the long-term car park was found to be the murder scene, then the camera on the floodlight in the long-term car park that she had spotted, might provide critically important information. Metal detectors could then be deployed more extensively to search the stream and adjacent grasslands for the murder weapon. The bullet hole strongly indicates a firearm as the murder weapon but the amount of blood discovered beside the stream could suggest a knife was also involved. Other evidence might rest in the stream –

particularly if the body was thrown in or crawled in to it - such as jewellery or even a purse. It is shallow, gently flowing, and rocky so it was well worth deploying significant resources there.

All of these permutations and combinations were buzzing around AJ's head as she neared the end of the beach with Gordon Lightfoot's *Sundown* pushing her on. She was feeling strong physically, so much so that maybe the November Clontarf Half Marathon that Ray was encouraging her to register for was achievable. When she complained that it was too long, he reassured her that participants were allowed to switch to the 10 km distance on the day, but not the other way around. Mentally, she was also grateful for the opportunity to clear her head and analyse things without anybody asking or answering questions. The loneliness of the long distance runner for her was a myth, she wasn't lonely at all. Quite the contrary, the solitude of the long distance runner was her mantra. She resolved to text Hennessy when she got home and suggest an early morning meeting at the airport to compare notes and agree the next steps. He might also have some news from his update session with Brophy. If no additional resources were forthcoming, she would try to establish if Lennon had made his request to Hennessy about doing some desk research when he got out of hospital. Although it wasn't exactly legit from a policy perspective, Lennon would feel a lot less guilty if he could do it and the investigation could only benefit, even if he found nothing. There again, she was pretty sure that Hennessy was unlikely to approve anything that could go badly for him, especially now that his self-esteem and confidence seemed to have taken a knock from the gunshot he suffered in the line of duty. Before that he was still concerned with correct procedures but his ego and self-confidence was such that he could have seen such a move as bravado and macho on his part.

Much would be revealed in the very near future she figured as she rounded the last bend in the now fading light and turned for home.

Refreshed. Positive. Expectant.

And still smiling.

Chapter 26

Norman Prendergast was sitting in the small, square, cluttered office at the back of his shop staring at the round, plastic clock on the wall opposite. Aside from being cheap and dirty, the clock looked disinterested, as if it had no particular desire in telling the time. The office's light green paint was peeling off the walls and the white ceiling had patches of damp generously scattered around it. An extravagant chandelier hung from the ceiling, only because several prisms were missing, rendering it unsellable. A large old-fashioned, brass safe dominated one wall. Some of the assorted art leaning against walls and on top of shelves appeared valuable, others looked cheap, and quite a few were clearly broken. Set against such disorder, his desk was surprisingly tidy. There was an old style dial-up black phone in one corner, an open diary opposite, a brown leather desk pad in front of the seat, and an ornate gold fountain pen neatly laid parallel to the desk pad. This was Prendergast's private space, his office man cave, where he went to be alone. His staff knew not to bother him there, not that they would have this afternoon as he had given the one assistant scheduled to work the day off. The pandemic had put an end to walk-ins and the only time customers made appointments nowadays was in the few days preceding an auction.

It was the last auction that was on his mind as he continued to gaze at the clock. The surprise bidder had unnerved him, upset his plan, and perhaps his reaction was too hasty, ill-judged even. Since he had taken an interest in this industry, and went on to forge a career in it, he noticed his propensity to experience adrenaline surges at the prospect of making lucrative deals had increased considerably. Such surges weren't the problem *per se*, it was the actions he took to complete those lucrative deals that were becoming a problem. It was as if he was careering down a dark tunnel that had no exits, and no light at the end of it, only a more absorbing shade of darkness. His life choices were getting more dangerous, not because of a limit in his choices so much as the limits he was imposing on those choices.

He wasn't stupid enough to consider himself a victim but the pattern was a familiar one. Poor decisions, often involving life-changing consequences for others, followed by a gargantuan rush as deals were closed, then reflection accompanied by varying levels of questioning and / or self-loathing. Commitments to reform lasted as long as a politician's promises or, in his case, until the next opportunity to make a killing came along.

It was what it was he told himself as he checked the time on his expensive wristwatch against the reticent wall clock. The single knock on his half-open office door was combined with its provider taking a seat opposite Prendergast, the office now over capacity.

'You're late'.

'Fuck does it matter, keeping you from something?' answered the guest.

'Then again, you never were one for punctuality, used to get me into trouble with mom and her six o'clock dinner time deadline back in the day' sighed Prendergast.

'Love to sit here and reminisce but tell someone who gives a fuck'.

'Or at owning up come to that. When she found your porn mags - what were they called *gerbil* or *hamster* or something - you stayed shtum and we both got into trouble'.

'Have you got it?' demanded the visitor tersely.

There was a deliberate pause from Prendergast as he looked down at his hands, now positioned gingerly on the desk.

'Not at the moment'.

'The fuck you sayin'?' stormed his visitor, standing up abruptly and knocking over the plastic chair, neck tattoo clearly convulsing.

Prendergast half stood up himself, raising both hands in a sign of both admission of guilt and attempt at placation.

'I will have, I just need more time' he answered in as soothing a tone as he could muster, given the fact that the room had now filled with aggression.

'It's not the kind of thing you can just whistle up ya know' continued Prendergast. 'I will have it, I guarantee you. It will just take a little bit longer'.

'Price has just gone up' stated the visitor, still standing up.

'Hold on, hold on' said Prendergast trying not to show any fear but knowing that violence came easy to his visitor. He recalled their family pet collie, *Kim*, getting kicked regularly and once having a mark under his eye that looked every bit like a burn. His mother loved that dog even though she pretended not to. Such cruelty made his stomach churn at the time and yet now Prendergast himself was responsible for much worse damage being inflicted on human beings. Even though Prendergast didn't personally carry out the action, that was no excuse, he was pretty sure he knew who the bigger monster was.

'Let's be reasonable here, it's a big prize after all. I would have contacted you to let you know but I wanted to talk to you about something else anyway'.

His visitor had an impassive expression.

'Did you know she's in hospital?' continued Prendergast.

The visitor gazed down at him contemptuously before answering.

'I heard'.

'She's asking to see you'.

No reply.

'This is it, she's done, it's brain cancer' pleaded Prendergast, pleased at least that he was getting a conversation going and that he was deflecting from the threat of violence, albeit temporarily.

'Look' Prendergast continued, 'I know it didn't end well between you two but – '

'You know fuck all' interrupted the visitor.

Maybe this was a bad idea Prendergast was quickly thinking to himself. Why am I using my salesman babble to change a topic that was looking like it was going to get me assaulted to a topic that now looks like it could get me assaulted? But he needed to get the upper hand here, by any means possible.

He decided to let some time pass and see if his visitor would add anything further. It gave him time to think. When there was nothing forthcoming, he decided to speak.

'Anyway, I said I'd ask but if – '.

'I'll be in touch with the new price, the final fucking price!' growled his visitor as he stormed out of the office.

Chapter 27

When AJ walked in to the conference room in the Garda station at Dublin Airport, she was surprised to see Hennessy already there, folders set out in front of him, head down, white face mask half covering his phone on the table, and his navy blazer neatly hung on the back of the chair beside him. Normally, AJ would stop to talk to one of the station officers on the way in and they would let her know if there was anyone already in the room but this morning the only officer on duty was dealing with a customer at the public counter.

'Morning Gar, no flies on you' greeted AJ cheerily.

'Good morning. I have to be in early to keep up with you' Hennessy responded in a half serious, half joking tone.

'The reason I texted you last night Gar – '

'I'm glad you suggested it AJ' interrupted Hennessy, 'it was exactly what we needed: to sit down and see where we're at'.

'Great' replied AJ hanging up her jacket on the coat stand.

'Let's start with structure, it's going to change' stated Hennessy.

AJ pulled her seat in and gave him a puzzled look.

'Brophy isn't well, she's off this case; in fact she's off all cases for the foreseeable future'.

An empathetic expression replaced AJ's puzzled one.

'She has cancer and as you probably know, there were rumours circulating for a while now about retiring so she might not be back at all' continued Hennessy.

'I'm sorry to hear that, so you now report to?' asked AJ.

'No idea'.

AJ's puzzled look returned.

'They were supposed to announce it before I met her but it was held up, she didn't know why' replied Hennessy.

'So it must be the Chief Superintendent, at least until you hear otherwise?' suggested AJ.

'I guess so but that's not my priority for the moment. My priority is to do what you proposed in your text: see where we're at and where we're going'.

'Let's start with Campbell shall we?' asked Hennessy as he scrolled numbers on his phone and pressed one. 'If she's so enthusiastic and ambitious she should be at work now, or at least answering her phone'.

Both detectives could hear Campbell's phone ringing. AJ peered out the window while they waited and was surprised to see that construction had started on the new Garda building. The site had been earmarked for a new station years ago but it struck AJ as strange that they'd begin the work during the Covid-19 pandemic with newspaper articles regularly reporting that the virus could put people off flying, particularly because air travel facilitated the spread of diseases.

After waiting over a minute, Hennessy hung up and muffled an expletive-laden sentence that AJ couldn't entirely decipher but got the gist of.

Outside, an aircraft landing made sufficient noise to maintain the silence in the room for another thirty seconds. Just as Hennessy was about to re-commence the meeting, his phone rang. When he saw Aoife Campbell's name he put it on speaker.

'Detective Inspector Hennessy, STO Campbell here. Apologies, I was finalising something in the lab and I missed your call but I have good news: the blood samples match' said an excited Campbell.

Hennessy and AJ looked wide-eyed at each other.

'Just to be clear Aoife. You're saying that the blood found on the grass at the airport car park site matches the blood from our victim?'

'Yes, no question Detective, they're a match. I can also tell you that there was only one type of blood found so far – we still have to test the items we found onsite - which strongly suggests we're only dealing with one person, your victim' gushed Campbell.

Hennessy continued to stare at AJ whilst he digested the information, before responding.

'That helps a lot Aoife, thank you. So you'll continue to search the stream and banks for more evidence?'

'Already on it Detective' answered Campbell.

'Great' said an impressed Hennessy. 'I'll ring Santry, they've been guarding the scene, and get more people there'.

'Two scenes, murder and disposal; there's gotta be a transport one at least in between?' asked AJ, almost to herself.

'And a stay in the stream combined with the warm weather might explain the rapid decomposition' said Hennessy.

'But how did she get in the stream, hardly crawled in with a bullet in her skull, which means the killer must have thrown her in but then – '

'Why take her out again and dump her in the construction site?' interrupted Hennessy.

'Maybe he got spooked, thought someone saw him or he decided she'd be found too easily?' theorised AJ.

Hennessy shrugged, flicking his pen in his hand and wanting to start writing something but not sure what to write.

'I need to ring Santry. And Lubenski, if we can tie down time of death – '

'We can check the CCTV footage' interrupted AJ, 'and who knows, maybe the floodlight camera in the car park was what spooked him?'

Chapter 28

Campbell was delighted to see the additional Garda resources deployed to the Cuckoo stream murder scene when she arrived back. She was even more pleased with the role she was now playing in this investigation. Informing Hennessy of the initial test results from the evidence collected here was one of the most exciting things she had done since joining the Technical Bureau. The staff shortage in the office was working out to her career advantage, as she had wanted. This was field experience at the front line and she was going to make the most of it. Starting with her next task: searching the stream and its environs for more evidence. If she could find anything else, it would surely cement her career profile in terms of seeking promotion.

She parked beside the Bureau van, put on her protective clothing, and joined her two technical colleagues already on site to get updates. It was a sunny, warm day and she knew she would be too hot in her white overalls just as soon as she started walking. The colleagues had started their work at the same point, with one proceeding upstream and one downstream. They would then move on to the adjoining western bank and converge again before finally tackling the bank on the eastern side of the stream. The metal detectors they were using worked both on land and underwater and were relatively recent in technology so they had large search coils, used pulse induction detection, and had built in high quality audio components to assist in submerged detection work. Campbell spoke briefly to the Garda Sergeant on site who confirmed that his officers were conducting visual searches using a grid system, assisted with poles for areas of thick undergrowth. So far, nothing of significance had been discovered.

Campbell was careful to approach her male colleague focussing on the upstream search from the side already covered by the metal detector. Her colleague turned off the detector and took off the headphones when she saw her.

'Anything so far?' asked Campbell.

'Absolutely zilch Aoife, not even a few coins that we'd normally get. I guess this is too isolated to have any kind of passing traffic' responded her colleague.

'How is the equipment performing?' probed Campbell.

'Fine, we did the standard test before we started and both detectors came through with flying colours'.

Campbell was standing in the middle of the stream as she conversed and found the bed quite rocky and unsteady.

'How deep does it get?'

'About twenty five centimetres at its deepest I'd say' answered her colleague.

'Not easy to keep your footing, is it?' suggested Campbell as she moved around a little. An aircraft coming in to land on the southern runway made everyone working at the crime scene look up and marvel at how clear they could see it, close enough to identify not just the airline but the name of the specific aircraft. Gazing around the exposed site and the continuous flow of vehicles on the nearby motorway and its even closer off-ramp from the M50, Campbell figured whatever happened here must have happened at night. Did that mean the perpetrators left more evidence than they wanted to simply because they couldn't see it, she wondered.

'It's not too bad, the flow is quite weak along this stretch so it doesn't knock you off-balance'.

'You've about another twenty metres to go before you move on to dry land?' queried Campbell looking at the bend in the stream where it went largely underground.

'About that. I reckon any chance we have of turning up something in the water will be downstream' said her colleague.

'Could be' replied Campbell, 'we're definitely missing parts of the mobile phone and maybe a few pieces of the reading glasses, not to mention a murder weapon. I'll head down to Liz, let me know'.

Campbell decided to wade through the water to get downstream and conduct her own visual inspection as she went. After all, not all murder weapons have metal components. She slipped twice on rocks that gave way as she went, the first time just about steadying herself without putting her hands down but the second time she was unable to re-balance quickly enough and was forced to put both hands on the river bank. A Garda with a search pole standing about ten metres away saw her trip and asked if she needed help. Trying not to look as ungainly as she felt she declined his offer but then felt something hard where her left, gloved hand had grabbed the grassy bank. She bent down to inspect her find more closely and gently pushed back pieces of grass from it. Still unable to establish what it was, she took a small penknife from her overalls and carefully prodded around a small mound about ten centimetres long. Her excitement level grew as the tip of the penknife confirmed that there was something metallic there. She was about to call one of her team to assist unearthing the object but then decided it would look better to her superiors if she could take full credit for the find herself so she continued to cut around and prise it up with the penknife. After a minute or two, there was enough of it above ground to use her thumb and index finger to lever it clear of the entangled grass.

Shite she cursed as a rusty cutaway from one of the fence poles became clear, quickly dropping it and hoping that the over-observant Garda wasn't still looking at her.

A few minutes later Campbell was getting the same unfruitful search results from her second team member on-site.

'If they did leave anything else around here, I don't think it's in the stream Aoife. Hopefully, we'll have better luck along the banks' said Liz.

'All we can do is try Liz. Is there another detector in the van, I'll give you a hand?' asked Campbell.

'No, we had four at one stage but someone must have borrowed or broken the other ones' responded Liz.

'Feck them anyway. I'll ring the office and see if they know'.

Campbell's call was answered after three rings by one of the lab analysts.

'No idea Aoife' replied the analyst who answered the call, 'I'll ask around but look, I've been continuing the tests on the bits of metal we found there -'

'Please tell me you've pulled a set of finger prints?' interrupted Campbell.

'Negative for prints I'm afraid Aoife' answered the analyst, 'but there's a decent blood sample on the temple of the broken reading glasses so I gave that in to the technicians to test for blood type and conduct DNA extraction. Then I swabbed the bridge and the nose pads – where there's no blood - to see if we can get enough material for a DNA profile. The idea being to compare it with the one from the blood and hence establish – hopefully using blood type and DNA – if the glasses belong to the victim'.

'Good work, well done, can you let me know about the metal detectors' said Campbell with a slight note of disappointment in her voice.

'Wait Aoife, it's about the blood on the temple of the glasses, I just got the results back' exclaimed the excited analyst, thinking correctly that Campbell was about to terminate the call.

Campbell listened attentively.

'It's not the victim's'.

Chapter 29

It's too much of a coincidence thought Fran Balfe as he peeked out from his dark antiques shop at the car park across the road. It's the same car, parked in almost the same spot, and containing two figures that he couldn't make out any details of. They definitely aren't waiting to collect someone from the pub a few doors up and he had never seen them drop anybody off so what were they doing?

Balfe's trip to the Garda station had been a total disaster as far as he could make out. He was nervous going in to make his missing person report but surely that was not unusual for someone with no experience of dealing with the police? Nor could it be that out of the ordinary for honest citizens filing such a report to appear even more stressed as the questions were put to him. The officer who spoke to him in the back office in particular gave the impression that he thought Balfe was lying through his teeth. But surely that's how they're trained to conduct such an interview he thought. Balfe wasn't clear about how many of the questions posed by the Garda were taken from the form he was filling in and how many were based on the suspicions that Balfe's responses were generating. Maybe it was possible to find one of those Missing Person's forms online so he could see for himself? At least he wasn't taken to an interview room; that would have made him feel even more anxious and look even more guilty of having committed a crime.

What if Balfe rang the station now and reported that the suspicious car that he told the officer about was parked across the road and that they could see for themselves that he wasn't lying and wasn't imagining it? They certainly didn't take it very seriously the first time. Balfe snuck another furtive look out through the side of the curtain to confirm that the car was still there as he pondered the situation. It hadn't moved. But what if he did ring, and the guards did arrive and question the car's occupants, and it turned out to be entirely innocent, how would he look then? Maybe the people in the car were tracking someone in the pub or maybe they were there at the behest of the pub, providing security in the event of any trouble inside? There could be lots of reasonable explanations. And even if there wasn't, it's not against the law to sit in a car outside an antiques shop or a pub or anywhere else. It might be suspicious but it's not illegal.

The more Balfe reflected on the different scenarios the more he concluded that he needed to know one way or the other. If they were well known antiques robbers then the appearance of the guards would surely have spooked them and if they were sitting there for legitimate reasons then it would set his mind at ease. Then he had another thought: what if they were undercover detectives from the drugs unit or the terrorist unit that the local station knew nothing about and his interference had jeopardised some major operation that was months in the planning?

Yes, leaving the guards out of it might be for the best he was now concluding. He had contemplated approaching the car himself when he first noticed it but that idea quickly lost its appeal when he considered the possibility of some form of roadside confrontation, resulting in him being abused or even worse, assaulted. He had witnessed several incidents outside the pub over the years, invariably at closing time involving inebriated customers, which started out as lively discussions and debates but quickly deteriorated into shouting matches and brawls. At the very least, asking the car's occupants their business there could lead to him being accused of behaving in too nosey a fashion for his own good and told to mind his own business. He found any type of aggression or hostility distasteful, always had.

Not that the guards in Dun Laoghaire seemed to believe that. How dare they ask him if he had hurt his wife, he was extremely concerned for her safety. He did know that husbands were obvious suspects when it came to domestic violence cases. In fact he had researched the statistics when he got home and was shocked to discover that half of female murder victims in Ireland were killed by a former or current male partner. What he found more difficult to establish however, was the percentage of those male partners who had backgrounds of previous violent behaviour towards women. He had no such history and he had no doubt the guards would have checked for any criminal record just as soon as he left the station.

Did that mean they would take his report seriously and do something about it, he asked himself as he climbed the stairs to his bedroom and left the car and its occupants – whatever their intentions - to their own devices. There was no minimum period of time that a person had to be missing for in Ireland before the guards commenced an investigation. That was the official policy but the appeals for information regarding specific individuals that Gardaí made to the public seemed to Balfe to fall in to one of three categories: teenagers, senior citizens who may have an illness such as dementia, and people known to be involved in some sort of criminal activity and whose disappearance may well be linked to same. Rebecca Balfe did not fall into any of those groupings, at least as far as her husband was aware.

When he switched off the light to turn in for the night he took one last look to see if the car was still there. It was.

But its occupants weren't.

Chapter 30

It felt better than just sitting around, that was for sure.

The kitchen table in the two-bedroomed, red-brick townhouse on the outskirts of Ballyboughal that Johnny Lennon shared with his girlfriend had a handful of folders scattered around a dark grey laptop and his mobile phone. Amongst the folders was a leaflet dropped in by the Ballyboughal Community Council informing locals of an upcoming advisory meeting with the Dublin Airport Authority concerning the flight paths and associated noise arising from the Northern Runway opening. The estimated completion time was about a year away. Aircraft pollution wasn't high on Lennon's list of priorities at the moment, particularly as they were renting the house and the lease was scheduled to expire at the end of the year. Rachel, his girlfriend, was a HR Trainer for a pharma company in nearby Swords and liked its proximity to work but she socialised in the city centre and didn't see it as a long-term prospect. Whether or not she saw Johnny as a long-term prospect was something he was unsure of.

The first answer he got - which he was expecting - was a flat no but a day after he got out of hospital, Hennessy rang and said he had changed his mind, proceeding to lay down the strict conditions under which Lennon could help the team out. Although he didn't say it, Lennon figured Hennessy must have spoken to the doctors and to his bosses, in that order, before changing his mind. The conditions included a maximum four days work a week and four hours a day with a minimum of thirty minutes break between each hour. He was also told to contact only Hennessy or AJ with any queries and to confine himself exclusively to desk research.

His laptop had access via a virtual private network to the Garda PULSE system, a central database used to record and categorise crimes. In addition, he could interrogate both Europol's Information System and Interpol's Criminal Information System online. Social media profiles were increasingly being used by policing authorities to assist investigations and he could easily look those up without any specific permissions. The folders surrounding the laptop were supplied by AJ and consisted mainly of hand written and typed notes and forms relating to the individuals that had been interviewed or identified as potential interviewees in respect of the case. Lennon wasn't sure if Hennessy knew that he had the paper files or if AJ had copied and provided them without informing him. Either way, Lennon found them extremely useful as some of the case information on PULSE was quite sketchy.

      The lung injuries sustained by Lennon were slowly healing but his breathing was still laboured at times, particularly when he went out with Rachel for a walk or climbed the stairs in the house too quickly. The dressings on the knife wound were changed by nursing staff three times a day when he was in hospital but he was changing them himself now once a day. The stitches themselves were self-dissolving but that would take one or two weeks and he was on strict instructions to attend the Day Care centre in Beaumont every week for a thorough check-up.

He was contacted by phone in hospital by the Garda's 24/7 Independent Counselling Service and strongly advised to consider availing of it considering the trauma that is experienced from such a serious incident. The letter and brochure that arrived the next day described very clearly how he could obtain immediate support from accredited counsellors over the phone and thereafter, if required, up to eight face-to-face sessions. The other free and confidential support services that he could utilise included the Chief Medical Officer, the Peer Support Network, and the Garda Employee Assistance Service. What Lennon wanted more than anything however was to get back to frontline duties but he realised that he wasn't physically – whatever about mentally – capable of doing that now. In the meanwhile, investigating the murder from the resources set out on his kitchen table would have to suffice.

The process he was employing to carrying out his task was based on chronological order. In other words, he was working through the individuals in the sequence that the inquiry team came across them, starting with the construction worker who reported finding the bones on the North Runway site.

Unfortunately, establishing if a particular person had a criminal record or not was a lot more complicated than simply typing in their name and waiting for their life story to appear instantaneously. For a start, people can change their name. They can also use pseudo-names or nicknames that may have been gleaned by detectives investigating a specific case but their original legal names may not always be known. Hence, for example, detectives may be told by several witness that a crime was committed by *'Dodger'* but they may have great difficulty ascertaining exactly who *Dodger* was. It might also be the case that several *Dodgers* are known to Gardaí but not necessarily the one referred to by witnesses.

Even the contrasting styles used by Hennessy and AJ in their notes gave Lennon an interesting insight into their different approaches and perspectives. What exactly could be recorded in such notes - as they could be legally obtained by defence teams - was an activity that he was well versed in from his training. Hennessy, for example, underlined the word 'eyesight' in his comments on the construction worker who reported the bones. Did that mean Hennessy didn't believe him or that the guy had very good vision, wondered Lennon as he considered if better sight might have prevented his stabbing. AJ on the other hand was more fulsome in her description of Matt Griffin, the man in charge of the fill dump for the runway: 'aggressive, covered in macho tats, used to dealing with us?' Turns out AJ was spot on; Matt Griffin had convictions for theft, assault, and selling stolen goods in Ireland and spent two years in an Italian prison for robbery. Did that suggest he was capable of murder or being an accomplice there to, scribbled Lennon in his own notes.

Some of the names on the long list that Hennessy and AJ gave him came across as squeaky clean, such as Cormac Tierney, the man who found the stream-side scene in the airport's long-term car park. He had never come to the attention of the guards and his online communications portrayed him as a family man who coached junior Gaelic games' teams and raised funds for charities on cycling trips. Other names, particularly the fifty plus construction workers from overseas who had access to the building and fill dump sites, had no records that he could find, be they criminal or otherwise. Construction staff and airport workers who had legitimate reasons for visiting the building areas constituted the vast majority of the names he was given. A few of them came up on his searches as victims of crime and that lead him to dig deeper as occasionally people who are subjected to a criminal act set out to seek revenge. For those dozen or so that came up with prosecutions against them, the most common reason was possession of drugs, invariably small quantities for personal use. It was a painstakingly slow process and he had to take regular breaks, not only because Hennessy had so instructed but because he found sitting down for prolonged periods uncomfortable to the point of being painful due to his injuries. It didn't help that he was finding desk research fairly boring and unrewarding. Nevertheless, he had to keep reassuring himself, it made him feel involved, if a little removed and lost.

Lennon's plan was to work his way through the list on an individual basis before starting phase two, which consisted of trying to find any connections between them, legal or otherwise. This cross-analysis procedure was designed to establish if people were holding vital information back, sometimes innocently. Shared addresses, hometowns, careers, industries, hobbies, holidays, bars, partners, friends, enemies, or prison cells might yield valuable information. Lennon was accustomed to looking for such traits amongst victims in his previous assignment: the people who fell prey to romance fraudsters were lonely, vulnerable, and reasonably or very wealthy. That was a critical missing component in this investigation of course: the identity of the murder victim. Assuming they do find that out, he would then delve into any linkages with her as phase three in his research.

He shifted in his seat to make himself more comfortable when AJ's name appeared on his phone.

'Hey Johnny, thought I'd check how you're getting on?' asked AJ.

'Good thanks AJ, in fact I was admiring your detective skills a while back. That aggressive bloke in the storage site that you thought had a record, he has'.

'Murder?' probed AJ.

'No but maybe a nice little resume for a budding killer' replied Lennon.

'Anyway, that's not why I'm ringing. How are *you* getting on?'

'Grand, not a bother' answered Lennon.

There was a pause before AJ said anything.

'Listen Johnny, that was a traumatic incident and a serious injury whatever way you look at it. Have the counselling services been in touch?'

'Sure, but I'm fine AJ. Except for the puncture that goddam shite-hawk left me with. I'm working away here, should be back on the frontline in no time'.

'Don't play the hard man Johnny, I've been there. It'll get into your head whether you like it or not. Next time you're confronting someone in a dangerous situation, it could make you doubt yourself, and that could get you, or much worse, me hurt. Either way, you'll need a medical cert before they'll let you out again'.

'You got stabbed?' queried Lennon.

'No, but I got shot at and fired a sidearm' explained AJ.

'A few times I hear?' probed Lennon.

'Whatever' said AJ after a moment. 'You need to reach out. It's nothing to be ashamed, the counsellors are excellent at their job and it's guaranteed confidential. Johnny, there's about two and a half thousand detectives on the force and you know how many have been stabbed? I'd say fifty, max. You could get a Scott Medal for fuck's sake!'

'Even fewer have been shot at,' commented Lennon, 'or fired a weapon'.

AJ didn't respond.

'The two project managers on the runway construction, you didn't meet them?' queried Lennon changing the subject when AJ wasn't saying anything.

'Nope' responded AJ in a clearly frustrated tone.

'Figured, there was nothing in your notes about them' said Lennon.

'What about them?' asked AJ, giving up on offering advice to Lennon.

'Well, the Irish one, O'Leary. He's been arrested a few times about burglaries but never charged, fairly recently as well'.

'Not exactly homicide' said AJ in a dismissive voice.

'S'pose so, just caught my attention as a bit unusual is all' said Lennon.

'Why, what did we think he stole?' probed AJ.

'Not sure, but something valuable I reckon, he was brought in by the Stolen Arts and Antiques Unit'.

Chapter 31

'You must be here about the arrests?'

'Eh, no. Are you Fran Balfe?'

'Yes?'

'I'm Detective Inspector Hennessy and this is Detective Jenkinson. We're here about the missing person report you filed, may we come in?' asked Hennessy as he and AJ donned face masks.

A worried Fran Balfe waved them into the shop and closed the front door.

'Have you found her, is she all right?'

'We'd like to ask you a few more questions to help with that if we may Mr. Balfe?' asked Hennessy.

'Oh, I thought you must have found her, you're very senior police' said a still nervous Balfe.

'We have your report here Mr. Balfe' said AJ in an attempt to steer him away from looking for a direct answer, 'could you clarify a few points please?'

'I've already gone over that in the station, twice in fact, once at the public counter and then inside with an officer called Stephen' answered Balfe.

'Yes, we know that Mr. Balfe and we know your wife isn't on any medication that you know of, doesn't suffer from any illnesses that you know of, didn't display any change in behaviour recently that you noticed, etcetera, etcetera. We see that Mrs. Balfe regularly travelled overseas to buy new merchandise for your shop here but it would help if we could get more detailed information about those trips. For example, who did she do business with?' queried AJ.

'You mean who she bought from overseas?

'Exactly, if we could get a list, not just overseas suppliers but here at home as well' clarified AJ.

'And a list of customers also please Mr. Balfe' interrupted Hennessy.

'I've already contacted the overseas vendors she frequented, it got me nowhere' said Balfe.

'From what I understand Mr. Balfe, your wife often purchased from markets?' asked AJ.

'Correct' answered Balfe, in a tone that suggested 'so?'

'Well, antiques markets in Asia have dozens if not hundreds of stalls'.

'So?' said Balfe, aloud this time.

'So you wouldn't necessarily be aware of all of the people your wife bought goods from, particularly if she had a tendency to use cash. I'm taking it the paperwork associated with cash sales might be a little scant?' probed AJ.

Balfe needed to steady himself before he replied to that. Maybe these detectives were linked to the Revenue and were really here to check his tax affairs, using the disappearance of his wife as a subterfuge?

Hennessy noticed Balfe's reticence and moved to allay any financial concerns he had.

'We're not interested in the paperwork Mr. Balfe, we just want to find your wife so if you could compile a listing of all of the buyers and sellers whatever their location that you and your wife interacted with, we would really appreciate it?'

Although he wasn't sure he believed them, Balfe seized the opportunity to be cooperative.

'That could take some time detective but I'll certainty have a go'.

'Could you print it out from your accounts Mr. Balfe, along with any contact details you have for them please?' asked AJ gazing over at the paperwork surrounding the laptop on the desk.

'Even if it wasn't complete initially, it would get us started and you could add to it as you went?' added Hennessy.

'Yes detective, that should be possible. I just need to make sure I'm not breaking any rules, you know, GDPR and all that'.

'Absolutely Mr. Balfe. If it would help, we can get a Court Order to release them?' said AJ.

'That shouldn't be necessary detective, I'll just give my solicitor a quick call. Some of our clients are quite secretive when it comes to their business dealings' said Balfe.

The two detectives looked at him.

'Not that they're hiding anything from the tax authorities of course', he went on, 'they just prefer privacy'.

'Would you like us to wait?' asked Hennessy.

'I'm not sure I can get him now, he's often in court. I have his number upstairs' said Balfe making his way towards the stairs. 'Please, take a seat at the desk, I should only be a few minutes'.

'One other thing please Mr. Balfe, as you're going upstairs, could we get a hairbrush or toothbrush belonging to your wife, just to make sure we have her DNA on file?' requested Hennessy, immediately regretting giving the impression that his wife was dead.

'It's standard procedure in missing person cases Mr. Balfe, allows us to rule out people' said AJ seeing the alarm in Balfe's eyes.

Balfe muttered something and continued on up the stairs.

The two detectives sat at the desk and stared at each other. They were conscious that there was most likely a CCTV system in the shop so they didn't say anything. They browsed the products on show as they waited. The showroom had a dark, impersonal vibe to it from AJ's brief assessment; the items on display didn't seem to have a lot of love shown to them and there was a cluttered, uncaring look to their presentation. Then again she thought, maybe that's deliberate in this business and the discerning buyer cared not a jot about the merchandising, concerned only with the specific piece that they came to inspect. That was the other thing that struck AJ as unusual compared to the retail outlets she frequented: there were no prices. Hennessy was busy texting while she continued her saunter.

After a few minutes, Balfe came down and said his solicitor wasn't available but he left a message and would contact the detectives as soon as he got advice. He handed Hennessy a plastic bag that resembled the ones air passengers used to show their liquids at security screening.

'This is my wife's toothbrush'.

Before Hennessy could answer him, AJ cut in.

'Could you give us some indication please Mr. Balfe of the quantity of cash your wife might usually carry for her overseas buying missions; also, you provided your wife's mobile phone number but the make and model details can be helpful?'

Balfe looked a bit surprised by the questions but AJ spoke again before he could answer.

'Sorry, while I think of it, the photograph of your wife attached to the report you completed looked like a passport pose; did your wife wear contact lenses...or maybe spectacles?'

Even Hennessy appeared a bit taken aback by the flow of questions now but he was impressed nonetheless at the subtlety his colleague showed in disguising the key pieces of information they needed to match the evidence that they had collected.

'My wife wears glasses for reading and driving, that sort of thing, and for using her mobile but she rarely uses her mobile phone and regularly loses it, so I'm never really sure what make or model she has at any particular point in time. She does try to keep the same number however, but as I say she only uses it occasionally, researching pieces that she spots in the markets, rest of the time it's turned off' answered Balfe, deliberately ignoring the question on cash.

'That's very helpful Mr. Balfe, thank you, and the amount of cash she brought...thousands...tens of thousands?' asked Hennessy to give AJ a break.

'Oh, it varied' hesitated Balfe, 'but usually thousands'.

Hennessy wanted to press him to be more precise but he didn't want to scare him, not at this point anyway. Balfe appeared anxious to usher the two officers to the door.

'Can I ask you for clarification on one other thing please Mr. Balfe?' asked AJ. 'You said your wife had no enemies; have either of you had any disagreements with business acquaintances, recently or at any time in the past?'

Balfe didn't answer immediately, pondering again if it was some kind of tax-related query.

'You know the type of situation that can arise Mr. Balfe, a buyer thinks they were overcharged or a supplier thinks they undercharged. Or maybe you or your wife felt cheated by the price or quality of some product?' clarified Hennessy.

'No, nothing like that' responded Balfe after thinking about it.

'Might it have happened overseas with your wife's business connections?' probed AJ.

'I'm sure my wife would have told me detective' said Balfe in a less than convincing voice.

As they left the shop, AJ remembered the obvious question they hadn't asked.

'You mentioned 'arrests' when we called, what arrests?'

'Oh, last night I reported two suspicious characters hanging around outside to Dun Laoghaire station and they sent a squad car. I saw them put someone in the back and one of the guards gave me the thumbs up. I assumed they arrested them and you were here to follow it up?'

Hennessy tried to hide from Balfe the bemused look he gave AJ.

'I saw the alarm box when we were coming in, was it on?' asked AJ.

'Absolutely, it's always on when we're closed, and the safe has a separate, monitored alarm'.

'Have you had any burglaries or attempted burglaries before?' probed AJ.

'Never'.

The walk back to the car made for an interesting conversation between the two officers.

'What kind of fucking idiots would try to break into a place with two alarms?' asked Hennessy.

'Dunno but I'll follow it up with Dun Laoghaire' answered AJ.

'Anyway, looks like Lubenski's office was right to contact us about the missing person report, our murder victim may very well be Rebecca Balfe' opined Hennessy.

'Could be, and that might mean a connection with the arrests. Balfe's report did mention suspicious people sitting in a car across the road' said AJ.

'Then there's the different blood type found on the glasses by Campbell's lab' said Hennessy as he opened the car door.

AJ took a breath before responding.

'Maybe we should have got Fran Balfe's toothbrush as well?'

Chapter 32

The Airport Police Control room was a familiar location to AJ but the two officers on duty were new to her. One of the officers was new to the Control room, having recently joined the organisation. She was being trained on how to use the equipment as AJ got to work. The artificial lighting in the room was designed to provide bright illumination continuously. This helped to create a sense of alertness for staff throughout their shift. For the same reason the chairs had stiff, upright, non-adjustable backs; the emphasis being on attentiveness rather than relaxation. Facial recognition technology was still not approved for use by security services in the country – at least not officially – so the vigilance of the officers monitoring the bank of screens in front of them was crucial to the effective policing of the airport. It wasn't just faces that were of interest of course, any suspicious behaviour – be it from an individual or vehicle or in some cases an unattended suitcase – attracted further investigation. In addition, the smooth flow of passengers, baggage and vehicles could be assisted by officers spotting build ups at the various processors and acting accordingly. One of the most regular interventions required by the Airport Police was road traffic accidents on the airport campus. Long traffic jams could develop quickly and tempers could become frayed when passengers were trying to catch a flight or get home after a trip. Officers knew from their training that adrenalin levels ran high for airport users – both arriving and departing – and that clearing any blockages was a high priority.

    Cognizant that she was making two large assumptions, AJ thought it was still worth a try to use the date that Rebecca Balfe was scheduled to fly out of Dublin Airport as the point to watch footage from the car park camera. If it turned out that Rebecca Balfe was not the slain woman, AJ was wasting her time. That was the first assumption. Whoever was responsible for the crime scene at the rear of the car park may not have accessed the site via the car park. That was the second assumption. With two motorways converging on the other side of the Cuckoo stream, it was certainly feasible to approach the location where all the blood stains were found without using the car park. In fact, it would be safer in many ways to avoid the car park given the cameras at the entrance, exit and throughout the parking zones.

    AJ was reflecting on these points as she flicked through the recordings, adept at this point in using the system on her own. Whilst the airport Garda station did have the ability to use the CCTV system live, it was quite convoluted to set up historical footage and involved making a request to the Airport Police. Moreover, the monitors in the Control room allowed for multi-cam viewing so that the same area could be looked at simultaneously from different positions. Hence, AJ found it easier and more productive to conduct her work there. She also liked interacting with the Airport Police as she found it made both their jobs easier. Sitting far enough away from the two officers on duty that she didn't have to wear a face mask, she made several requests – mainly related to cameras by zone - to the experienced officer as she worked.

    The fact that the cameras were positioned to focus on what was happening inside the car park rather than outside was expected by AJ. She knew the high camera that she spotted could not have captured whatever happened on the bank of the stream but her hope was that the people involved came through the car park. The records maintained by the airport had already confirmed that the registration of Rebecca Balfe's car had not been picked up but there could be many reasons for that they explained, both deliberate and accidental. Dirty registrations plates, fake plates, frosted plate covers, and spraying illuminated glitter on the plate's characters all had the potential for a failed reading. Sometimes, the camera lenses at the entrance and exit could be dirty, again either maliciously or accidentally. That news came as a big disappointment to AJ as an image of the car might also pick out the occupants. The vehicle was now listed as stolen but AJ knew that the Red park alone had some eight thousand car spaces and overall airport car parking capacity for the public was over twenty thousand and rising. Therefore, even if the car had been parked here, finding it would require significant resources. At some point however, AJ considered that as an option to be revisited, if they were making no progress with other aspects of the investigation.

As darkness fell in the pictures on the monitor in front of her, the high rise camera was finding it difficult to display clear images, despite the strong floodlighting in the car park. AJ was able to speed up the replay but still found this activity quite time-consuming and boring. She wondered if there was any way to get Lennon or someone else to do it; the lack of resources on this case was taking its toll. There were no hard and fast rules about how many detectives should be assigned to a murder case, she knew that only too well. When she was based in Limerick – ironically working alongside Hennessy – homicides involving the feuding drug gangs had almost unlimited manpower but such was the nature of the tit-for-tat killings at the time, teams were invariably examining several related cases at the same time. In one particular example that concerned two men walking through the city centre on a Monday afternoon being assassinated by a lone gunman who made his getaway on foot, she recalled over thirty detectives being assigned and over twenty five thousand hours of CCTV footage having to be trawled through. The other experience she had of an abundance of resources being made available for a murder inquiry was when a seven-year-old girl was viciously abducted and here body found two lays later in a forest. That case left an indelible mark not just on AJ but on all the officers who were involved, particularly those who had children. The slain girl's older sister had been the last one to see her and felt inconsolable guilt for not taking more care of her. Family liaison officers and counsellors assigned to the inquiry were present at the family home every time AJ visited to interview family members but they struggled to comfort that older sister. As an only child, AJ had no understanding of sibling relationships and needed advice from the professionals before she attempted to glean more information from the sister. That was before the Gardaí introduced specialised training for conducting interviews with minors. Now it was standard practice to call in the specialised officers from the start.

The only interesting behaviour that her inspection of the car park tapes had revealed so far was the number of people who parked their cars and immediately sought out a suitable location to relieve themselves. She supposed it was because of the distances customers had travelled but there again, they had all passed by the public toilets at the entrance.

Nor was it necessarily a bad thing she reflected, as the crime scene was discovered by just such a passenger. One individual that looked to be engaged in that activity turned out to be vomiting when AJ zoomed in on them among the shadows, not trying to invade their privacy but rather checking if they were close enough to the crime scene to have seen anything. Another couple had unloaded their baggage from the back of the car and proceeded to the bus pick-up point with one suitcase clearly left behind. On a few occasions, passengers had disembarked the bus and walked around searching for their car, in one case for fifteen minutes. Parking in daylight and returning at night could make for a big difference.

After two hours – when her eyes were seeing dots – she took a break and stretched her legs in the corridor outside the Control room. She was always amazed at how well insulated the Control room was when she re-emerged from it. Immediately the hustle and bustle of people and noise of aircraft hit her. Even with the lower passenger numbers because of the Covid pandemic, there was a continuous flow of people moving towards the departure gates. Some were wearing face masks, most seemed a little agitated, and there were a few that were downright stressed out as they hurriedly pushed past other passengers, presumably for fear of missing their flight. AJ walked along the corridor, took in the natural light and the fresher air, and pondered her next move if the date she was concentrating her efforts on drew a blank.

The text from Hennessy was good news: *Balfe is giving us names. I gave him Lennon's email.* She would have preferred to hear that the DNA from Rebecca Balfe's toothbrush matched that of the victim but she realised that the process took time. Maybe she should tell Lennon that checking the names before they got the results could turn out to be a waste of time but he should have copped that himself, he is a detective after all.

A shift change had taken place when AJ resumed her search duties in the Control room and the new officer – who she recognised to say hello to but, like so many other Airport Police staff, had no idea of the name – was more chatty.

'Any news on the murder inquiry?' asked the officer.

'No arrests yet but we're making headway' lied AJ.

'Did you identify the victim?' he probed.

'Working on it' answered AJ, leaning closer in to the screen to make it more obvious that she needed to focus.

'D'ya reckon it was an inside job, you know, one of the construction people?'

AJ glared over at him, deciding if he was just making conversation, trying to be helpful, or making a point that the airport's rumour mills were reporting no significant headway in the investigation. There again, it would be widely known – particularly among the Airport Police – that a second crime scene had been discovered in the long-term car park. She was also attempting to gauge if the atmosphere in the room had changed in the last few seconds, if this officer had been discussing her presence with his colleague when she was taking a break, if the level of comradery and collaboration that she thought was present when she first arrived had been replaced with a more forbidding tone, if the glossy walls had paused their task of deflecting light while they awaited an outcome.

'Why do you say that?' she eventually replied, making sure there was a slightly defiant edge to her voice.

He seemed unsure about what he was saying when he was put on the spot.

'Well, you know....access to where you found the bones being restricted...the argy- bargy between the workers there...that sort of thing'

'So one of the construction people has been reported missing?' probed AJ.

'Not that I know of, no' clarified the officer promptly, backtracking.

'You don't suppose we might have checked that or that the companies might have told us that one of their staff went missing a few weeks ago?' queried AJ at the same time as hoping that Hennessy had asked them that. Of course he would have, he's an experienced detective she reassured herself.

'For sure you would, sorry, just trying to make small talk. Let me know if I can help with anything there' responded the officer, retreating behind his own monitor now.

It did set AJ thinking however. What if the victim was related to the construction of the new runway? Would the team have known about someone not turning up for work recently? Would a woman in her sixties be involved in the project? Had Lubenski specifically stated the ethnicity of the victim? Could he tell that from the material he was working with? And what about her discussion with Dun Laoghaire station about the arrest Balfe mentioned? Balfe said there were two suspicious characters repeatedly sitting across the road in a car but only one person was arrested by the officers who responded and there was no sign of a suspicious car. What made it worse was that the man who was arrested hadn't actually broken any laws – he said he just went for a stroll while he was waiting for someone to come out of the pub - so he was released without charge and told to keep away from the area. AJ had been given the name and address that he provided but the address didn't exist and there was no record of the name - which looked Scandinavian and which AJ doubted was genuine – having any criminal record. So was Balfe misinterpreting the whole suspicious car thing? If so, where did the second person that he claims he saw that night get to?

      Such was her degree of preoccupation with these questions, combined with the tedious nature of the task at hand, that she almost missed the scene playing out on the screen in front of her.

Two figures were carrying something heavy in the direction of the Cuckoo stream.

Chapter 33

Miriam Hennessy couldn't help smiling when she heard the front door gently opening and closing. She used to have a more relaxed approach to dealing with the potential dangers of her husband's chosen career but since the shooting....well, how could she not be concerned? It wasn't so bad when he returned to work on light duties, mainly desk-based, but since he had been put in charge of this murder case, her anxiety levels had gone way up. The routine that had developed with predictable meal times and regular hours was immediately ended. What if he's shot again she worried, and dies this time? Where does that leave her and their daughter Anais? It's all very well when he says he'll be extra careful, not take any risks, always have other detectives with him but she had heard all that before...and look how that worked out. The widow's pension for a fallen officer was far from reassuring; she didn't even want to know the numbers, the topic was too gruesome to contemplate. She had deliberately gone back to work as a nurse, on a part-time basis, to take her mind off the whole thing but the pandemic meant she was forced to do her job remotely, using a laptop provided by her employer. So most of her days were still spent at their cottage in Skerries and that was not a conducive environment to stop worrying about her husband. Anais was a typically active, energetic nineteen-year-old student who spent her days studying business at Dublin City University and her evenings socialising. Miriam didn't discuss the worries she had about Garoid going back to dangerous duties with Anais but she sensed that her daughter shared those concerns.

'Hi love, dinner nearly ready. What kind of day did you have?' she inquired from the kitchen, still wearing the orange exercise top and black leggings from a lunch-time cycle earlier. She was an attractive, sprightly woman in her early fifties with fair, shoulder-length hair and a bubbly personality.

'Great, same old stuff, nothing very exciting' replied Hennessy, making a conscious effort to make his job sound boring, and safe.

When he had locked away his revolver, he took his place at the small oak dining table and looked out the bay window at their neat but tiny garden, tended to by his wife. They had painted the dining room a light turquoise shade in order to maximise the sunlight and it was certainly working this evening as the sun slowly faded to close the warm sunny day.

As much as he tried these days to steer the conversation over dinner away from his work, Miriam invariably found a way to bring it up. Today, she used AJ for that purpose.

'How is Anna getting on, big help?'

'Yeah, she's very good, very thorough' answered her husband.

'So you've got over all of that hullaballoo in Limerick, whatever it was?' probed Miriam, knowing some of the background to their falling out over AJ shooting at a car they were chasing but never wanting to drill down into the detail of it.

'Yeah, we get on fine, working away' said Hennessy.

They continued eating while Miriam thought of another angle.

'Is she still single?'

Hennessy wasn't quite sure where this discussion was going but he hoped his wife wasn't thinking of any kind of romantic dimension.

'No, I think there's a guy on the scene. Think they have an apartment in Clontarf'.

'Good for her. You should invite them to dinner sometime. You know, just to be sociable?' suggested Miriam.

Only Hennessy would ever know how truly terrible an idea he thought that was, but he wasn't about to tell his wife that. He pretended to be still chewing on his food for another while.

'I dunno know Mir, mixing business and pleasure and all that...' feigned Hennessy.

Miriam now took extra long chews on her food. *Misophonia* was the term – she knew that because she had looked it up years ago – used to describe a behavioural trait that someone finds particularly irksome such as when her husband acted in this way: avoiding the issue she wanted to talk about. Grinding of teeth, fingernail-biting and eating with one's mouth open were other examples of misophonia that were listed in the article that she read on the subject but she was pleased to report that none of these applied to her husband.

'Maybe we should all go for a picnic this Saturday, get some of the Summer weather into us, what do you say Mir?' suggested Hennessy to break the silence.

'Anais has a study group in the morning and camogie practice in the afternoon' answered Miriam, not explicitly meaning to demonstrate how quickly her husband had forgotten their daughter's busy schedule but letting it hang there nonetheless.

It wasn't so much a tense air in the dining room now as an expectant one, as if a butterfly was flapping on the inside of the bay window and reacts excitedly to its opening.

'Is it just you and AJ then, working on the murder, is the new fella still out?' asked Miriam. If she was going to be the first to speak then by golly she was going to return to the investigation.

'No, not at all. We have a whole team of back-up people, medical experts, ballistics, laboratory technicians, scientists from different disciplines, it's a team approach and we've got a great team'.

'I mean the ones in the firing line, pun intended. You and AJ. Two, on a murder case? Look what happened to the new guy, not a full day there and he nearly gets murdered himself, Jesus Garoid!' pleaded Miriam.

'That was a freak incident Mir, and nothing to do with our inquiry. He was just in the wrong place at the wrong time. Plus, he's fine now, I have him doing some work at home before he comes back on frontline duty again' said Hennessy in what he hoped was a reassuring voice but he was cursing Lennon and the associated newspaper headlines about the stabbing at the same time.

Hennessy spooned himself some more chicken pie, not by way of distraction but rather because he loved his wife's way of making pies. They usually shared the cooking duties but he could never recreate her way of mixing different vegetables and sauces to get such appetising flavours. He offered his wife the dish but she declined.

'Brophy is sick'.

He said it with the same air as 'pass the salt please' but its impact on the room was like a deflating balloon whirling around in an uncontrolled manner whilst onlookers looked on in bemusement to see where it eventually landed. The imaginary balloon eventually landed beside Miriam.

'Your boss? What's wrong with her?' gasped Miriam.

'She didn't say but it sounds serious, had to have an operation' replied Hennessy.

'The poor woman. When will she be back?' probed Miriam.

'I'm not sure she's coming back. Rumour was she had been close to retiring'.

Numerous thoughts were mulling around in Miriam's head, competing for attention and vocalisation.

'So, she's had the operation? How did it go? Who's taking over? Are they expecting you to take over, wouldn't that mean you were off the streets and in an office?' asked Miriam, her excitement levels rising.

'I contacted the hospital but they just said she was in recovery, and she doesn't want any visitors.

None of the other stuff has been decided, at least as far as I know. I'm reporting in the interim to the next line up but he's taken on her duties on top on the stuff he was already doing so he just told me to carry on. My case is relatively low-level in the scheme of things cos there's no gang involvement' explained Hennessy.

'So effectively you're getting no supervision on the case? What about more detectives, have you asked? When will all of this be decided, surely they have a plan?'

Hennessy didn't want to get into a discussion with his wife about his last meeting with Brophy, when she thought she would have been in a position to brief him on the new arrangements, but seemingly was told she couldn't at the last minute. He knew that the organisation he had devoted his career to could act like that at times, it wasn't a huge surprise, par for the course in many ways. His wife, however, was not accustomed to that kind of carry on and he was not about to try to explain it or justify it or pass it off as standard practice. Miriam was more black and white than he was when it came to organisations and their machinations. She would want to know what Brophy had said and what her husband thought she might have been going to say. She would then move to what his interim boss had said, exactly, line by line. No matter how much he tried, Hennessy knew from experience that the discussion would disintegrate into him coming across as not asking his superiors enough questions and even more disconcerting from his point of view, as weak.

The notification on his phone was an email from Senior Technical Officer Aoife Campbell titled 'Report on testing of toothbrush obtained from Mr. Fran Balfe'. Hennessy politely told his wife that he had to read this and quickly scrolled down through all the technical information about how the tests were carried out until he arrived at the critical piece.

Result: Inconclusive.

Chapter 34

He was glad that he could do it by phone, rather than having to meet them. Clandestine meetings were all well and good as far as he was concerned when you were dealing with relatively upstanding individuals, criminal but otherwise upstanding, but the physical presence of the two individuals that had undertaken several nefarious operations on his behalf cast an unpleasant tang, that lingered long after their departure. Norman Prendergast had read the newspaper report of the assault that took place in Santry and was appalled at the photos of the knife injuries sustained by the two residents, notwithstanding the fact that he had instigated the break-in. Fortunately for him, nothing was mentioned about anything being stolen, something Prendergast believed was probably as a direct result of threats from their assailants to return, as the object in question was legally held. A Garda investigation into a theft from the property would inevitably have brought them to his door, as the agent who sold it.

The waiting and monitoring game wasn't working and with time being of the essence, he decided to take more explicit action.

Chapter 35

'DNA'.

'Camera'.

'DNA is unique, it's the gold standard'.

'Except for identical twins. Camera is a smoking gun, you have them committing the crime. Murderer, victim, weapon, location, all at the same time in the same shot. Done and dusted'.

'How often do we get that?'

'Not the point, point is which is better? CCTV, dashcam, mobile phones, loads of opportunity these days to catch a killer' explained Detective Johnny Lennon.

'Yeah but DNA – '

'You're not here Johnny' interrupted Hennessy as he strode into the airport station conference room for the update meeting he called with AJ and Johnny Lennon.

AJ turned to Johnny expecting to see a look of bemusement but he remained poker-faced. *He'll do well here* she thought.

'I've spoken to Campbell in Technical; the toothbrush we got from Balfe seems to have been washed with or fallen into some sort of bleach' Hennessy continued as he took a socially-distanced seat. 'Whether that was deliberate or accidental is unclear but I've asked the Sergeant in Dun Laoghaire to call up to him and get something else, a hair brush ideally'.

'Bleach suggests mischief?' ventured Lennon.

'Maybe, but hard to prove and we haven't time; we need to nail down as a matter of urgency if the victim is his wife or not' replied Hennessy.

'Did she have any update on the different blood found on the victim's glasses?' asked AJ.

'No match so far, you found two people on the car park footage pushing a bag?'

'Yeah, it's pretty murky though. I've sent the footage to Technical to see if they can blow up the images but I couldn't make out faces or what car they got out of or what they were pushing. This is the print-out' explained AJ handing out two A4 sheets to her colleagues.

The meeting paused as Hennessy and Lennon studied the picture. AJ looked around the bare walls of the room and tried not to think about how easily she could have been shot dead in it. Each time she visited it the memories became a little more bearable and a little less dark. She wondered if she could ever sit in it without experiencing these recollections. Telling herself that it was a good outcome, that she wasn't shot and that she downed the man chasing her, didn't seem to work at turning it into a positive reminiscence. She wondered if Hennessy had similar thoughts about the gunshot injuries he sustained when he passed through the car park adjacent to the station. Outside the sun was shining in between light showers and there was the distinctive if faint hum of an aircraft engine coming from somewhere on the nearby airfield. The cursed coronavirus was still having a destructive impact on air travel she mused before Lennon interrupted her daydreaming.

'That was a really good spot AJ, your eyes must have been burning from going through all that footage'.

'So that date and time' asked Hennessy before AJ could respond to Lennon and pointing to the numbers on the top right-hand side of the image, 'line up with when Rebecca Balfe was supposed to be going through the airport and they're about, what, ten metres away from the second crime scene?'

AJ nodded in the affirmative.

'The victim is Rebecca Balfe boss, hundred per cent' said Lennon in an assertive tone.

Hennessy was pensively stroking his beard with his left hand. After a few moments he gazed over inquisitively at AJ.

'I'm with Johnny, the missing person report matches the remains according to the medical people and the two crime scenes have been connected by the technical people. We can't match the pieces of mobile phone we found to her cos it seems she changed it regularly but she did wear reading glasses and we did find pieces of glasses. I recommend we should proceed on the basis that she's the victim until we get the DNA evidence, which will probably take another few days?' suggested AJ.

The thoughtful expression on Hennessy's face was turning to one of deep concentration. His eyes closed so tightly that AJ asked herself if he might still be getting spasms of pain from his wounds. She could sense Lennon staring over at her but she didn't acknowledge it. Hennessy sighed, hoping it wasn't as loud as he had heard it. There was no Brophy to advise or admonish him regarding the next steps and he didn't want to bother her stand-in about what should be a reasonably straightforward decision for a lead investigator on a murder case: if the evidence available points to a specific identity, follow that line of inquiry until you find out otherwise. When the other two detectives working on the case recommend that course of action, the decision becomes even more logical. Yet Hennessy found himself struggling with making it. It wasn't that he questioned the reasoning, it made perfect sense to him. What he was grappling with was his ability to make it. *You're a Detective Inspector for fuck's sake* he was scolding himself, *get your act together*. Ability wasn't the term he should be using though he told himself, what he was lacking was confidence. Why had his confidence deserted him now he pondered, and for such a piddly little decision? Almost sixty seconds had passed before Hennessy opened his eyes again and sat up straight in his seat.

'I agree, suspects?' He hoped his voice didn't sound as weak to his colleagues as it did to him.

'Balfe has to be up there' said AJ, 'even if he didn't deliberately mess up the toothbrush, partners are responsible for over half of female murders here'.

'For solved murders, but he did report her missing?' said Lennon.

'Wouldn't be the first to do that. Okay, let's take a closer look at Balfe. Johnny, you're going through the lists he's forwarding, include him in the background checks' said Hennessy, feeling more comfortable now.

'Hundred per cent boss' answered an eager Lennon, taking a note of it.

'The two guys you saw on the CCTV AJ' continued Hennessy.

'Can't even tell they're male but I'm following up with technical' replied AJ.

'Be handy if they're the two characters Balfe said were watching him?' suggested Hennessy.

'One of whom we arrested, and let go but yeah, assuming Balfe is telling the truth, it'd be a big coincidence if they're not the same' responded AJ.

'What if there was only one and that's him and Balfe carrying the body in the car park?' asked Lennon.

Lennon could see that the two detectives were considering his theory and was pleased with himself that he was making some kind of contribution, however obvious or implausible.

'We should get a hold of their life insurance, see if that's what motivated him' continued Lennon, on a roll now.

'Easy on' cautioned Hennessy before AJ could say it, 'we need a Court Order for that and we're a long way from meeting the threshold required. It was probably well known in that business that she carried a lot of cash so maybe it was a robbery gone wrong'.

AJ briefly saw the deflated look on Lennon's face before he put his head down and started scribbling something.

'What about the lists you're working on Johnny, you reckon the Irish construction guy might be worth a closer look?'

'Dylan O'Leary is his name, he's one of the project managers on the runway. The Stolen Arts Unit arrested him a few times for burglaries but he was never charged. I'm happy to follow it up with a call but you told me not to contact anyone but yourselves' answered Lennon looking at Hennessy.

'Correct, I met O'Leary so I'll talk to Stolen Arts, maybe you can come with me AJ? Johnny, I hope you're keeping to the hours I gave you?' said Hennessy.

'Hundred percent' replied Lennon, 'there's two sets of lists that I'm working on: the one from the case file of people you've interviewed or planned to interview, and the contacts you asked Balfe for. He's forwarding names but he's kind of drip-feeding them, a few at a time. I'm using our own systems first and if anything of interest pops up, I'm delving a bit deeper using social media. It's a slow process but I'm getting through it'.

'I appreciate that work Johnny and well done on spotting O'Leary but your health comes first. If you get tired at any stage, rest up, seriously' said Hennessy.

'Gar, if it is Rebecca Balfe and that's her body the two figures in the car park are pushing, we really should include all airport and construction staff who had access to the skeleton crime scene since that date. I've got a log of different CCTV camera positions from the Airport Police – the runway access gates used by construction traffic change as the work progresses so the cameras are moved accordingly – so that needs to be studied from that date as well and that's a shitload of work. The cameras on the car park entrance and exit need to be checked to see if they captured her or them coming or going, and then there's the matter of her car; did she use it, did they use it with fake plates, did they leave it in the car park and leave in a different car or did they leave across the fields at the Cuckoo stream? We need more staff' said AJ.

Hennessy was about to respond in a more self-assured tone this time when he noticed Lennon pushing back from the table and looking down at a dark stain slowly spreading across his stomach.

'Sorry folks, looks like my wound has re-opened'.

Chapter 36

The sign on the first door outside the lift read 'Anti-Racketeering Unit' as Hennessy and AJ continued along the third floor of Garda Headquarters in the Phoenix Park to the second door, the one they were looking for: Arts and Antiques Unit. They were both expecting a scene similar to Balfe's antiques shop in Killiney with dusty old pictures and pieces of furniture scattered haphazardly around the office but that image didn't last long as they gazed around a tidy but dated office with half a dozen desks ordered neatly along the three large wood-framed windows.

'Some of the desks might look like antiques but that's because they haven't been replaced for decades' commented Detective Sergeant Vincent Hargraves as he approached the two detectives with his hand out. 'Vinny, I spoke to you on the phone, take a seat'.

Hargraves had a round face, a goatee beard, a bald head and dressed in what could only be called un-smart casual with ill-fitting black jeans and an over-sized grey sweatshirt.

'Dylan O'Leary, I opened his file here' continued Hargraves as he sat in front of his computer monitor.

'Yeah, his name has come up in a murder inquiry' responded Hennessy.

'Well, I'm not sure if he's a murderer but we're fairly sure he's up to his bollix in stolen art, sorry about the language' said Hargraves looking at AJ. She didn't respond.

'But he's never been charged with anything?' probed Hennessy.

'Not yet, no but his name has come up a few times as someone who deals in stolen stuff, nothing too high-brow, statues and paintings mainly, we're talking about values from low hundreds to low thousands' expanded Hargraves.

'Does he steal it himself or sell it on?' asked AJ, adjusting her chair slightly so she could see his picture on the screen.

'Both' replied Hargraves confidently, 'and we think he's got aggressive with a few of the lowlifes he interacts with but, as I say, common assault grade rather than life-changing injuries or murder'.

'Strikes me as a bit unusual' said Hennessy thinking back to his interview with O'Leary, 'this guy has a fairly responsible and I'd say well-paid job; why would he be bothered mucking around with small time stolen art?'

'True, lives pretty modestly as well. We've searched his house twice and it's well fitted-out and everything but nothing suggesting an interest in antiques. There again, that's how a lot of the unscrupulous fuckers we deal with are; they might steal a painting worth a million but they don't show off any great wealth'.

'How do they get rid of it; are they stealing to order?' probed AJ.

'At the higher end, most of the time but at O'Leary's level, they sell it on to another fence and it turns up on some market stall or they flog it to a dealer' answered Hargraves.

'Do many antiques' dealers engage in stolen products?' probed AJ again.

'About a half dozen, ten at the most around the country I'd say'.

'Does the name Balfe ring a bell, husband and wife team run a place in Killiney called Village Antiques?' asked Hennessy.

'I've heard the name sure but they're not on our radar for dodgy dealings. I can give you a list of the ones we focus on' responded Hargraves.

As the meeting was ending, AJ looked at the five or six officers in the room and asked Hargraves about the size of the stolen art business in Ireland.

'In terms of the value of goods stolen here every year, probably in the millions, but globally it extends to cultural theft, forgeries, counterfeit, all kinds of shit, and sometimes that ends up here. This office is tiny – as is the racketeering unit next door – but Interpol and Europol have big numbers investigating massive organised crime thefts and scams. Every so often, we'll get notified that some big player – a dirty dealer or counterfeiter – is here and we might be asked to tail them or sometimes to detain them, to show we're watching them. We don't always know who the fuck they are or what the fuck they're up to, to be honest with you, but we have to be seen to be cooperating with the European boys'.

'Has that happened recently?' probed AJ as they stopped at the door.

'Funny you should ask that – and this has nothing to do with O'Leary, at least as far as we know – but Europol alerted us a few weeks back to this fence supposedly visiting here. They didn't ask us to do anything, it was just an information notice that they post, which usually means a low-level scumbag. Anyway, we put it up on our system in case she crosses our path. Usually, that's the end of it but lo and behold this woman's name turns up in a serious assault out in Santry' explains Hargraves.

'She assaulted someone?' queried Hennessy.

'Fuck no, herself and the guy she was with were nearly stabbed to death in the house they were renting. When I say stabbed, it was more like torture by cutting, gruesome shit. We didn't visit the house but apparently there was blood everywhere, looked like a fucking abattoir!' answered Hargraves.

'So they were stealing antiques or selling them?' asked AJ trying to make sense of the story.

'Fucked if I know, they wouldn't answer our questions when we interviewed them, scared shitless if you ask me. You should have seen them, bandaged up like fucking mummies they were. Santry detectives couldn't find any leads in the house, no fingerprints, nothing of value, it was rented, pretty rundown as I understand it. They're talking to the owner but I doubt it'll go anywhere...probably used false names...she has a lot of different names apparently'.

'So maybe it had nothing to do with stolen antiques?' suggested Hennessy.

'They were up to something alright, wasn't a burglary that went wrong, too severe' replied Hargraves.

'Are they still in hospital?' asked AJ.

'Should be, but fucked off during the night. Like I said, they were caught up in some sort of serious shit, I'm sure of it' responded Hargraves.

The two officers had the same thought at the same time but AJ got the question out first.

'This woman wasn't in her sixties and wore glasses by any chance?'

Chapter 37

Dun Laoghaire Garda station was about three kilometres from Killiney village, on the south side of Dublin city. When one of the sergeants stationed there, Noreen McKenna, got out of her patrol car outside the *Village Antiques* shop, she was struck by the picturesque view of Killiney bay and Bray head from the front of the shop. A keen swimmer, she regularly took a dip in Killiney beach or Sandycove's forty-foot before or after a shift. As the sun was shining and it was approaching two o'clock – the end of her shift - she decided there and then that Killiney beach would be her bathing venue of choice today.

Noreen was over twenty years in the force and coming up on five as a sergeant when she was transferred from Stradbally in County Laois to Dun Laoghaire during the pandemic. She checked that she had a small evidence bag but didn't bother taking a mask from the car as she didn't plan to go inside. It wasn't unusual to get a second or even third personal item for DNA purposes in the case of missing persons. She preferred hairbrushes herself as someone once told her that certain toothpastes could interfere with the sample on the toothbrush. Whether or not that had happened in this case, who knew, but a hairbrush was going to be her first request.

The closed sign was hanging on the inside of the front door so she pressed the bell and stood back. She couldn't see any lights on but it was lunchtime so maybe the owner was upstairs or had gone out for lunch. After a minute or two, she tried the bell again, holding it down a little longer this time. She knew that the detective who made the request was heading up a murder inquiry but didn't know if Balfe was aware that the victim might be his wife. She seemed to recall this shop name coming up recently in connection with suspicious people watching it but then again, most antiques and jewellery shops regularly reported being monitored. Noreen understood the angst that owners with valuable stock must experience when they think someone is planning an armed robbery. Several times she had responded to calls after such a robbery, the hysterical owners deriding the Gardaí for not taking their reports seriously.

Deciding that Balfe must have gone out for lunch, Noreen got back into her car, reversed out of the parking spot on to Killiney Hill road, and just as she was straightening the steering wheel to drive off, she noticed something. It was a slight twitch in the curtain of the middle upstairs window. The curtains were open and the sun was shining brightly on the window so she might have been imagining it or at the very least exaggerating it. Maybe there was someone there and it was Balfe himself she thought to herself as she pulled away slowly. He owns the place, he's allowed to peek out the window, particularly if he's not expecting a visit from the Gardaí. She had learned over the years that even the most law-abiding of folk were often reluctant to open the door when they saw a patrol car parked outside or the silhouette of a Garda at the front door. But then again, it was Balfe who reported his wife missing, and it was Balfe – as far as she could recall – who called in about being watched. Surely therefore she reasoned, bringing the car to a gentle stop, he would want to find out why she was ringing his doorbell.

Perhaps he couldn't see the front door from upstairs and when he saw it was the guards, he would come downstairs and open the door. She looked in her rear-view mirror for any sign of the door opening, conscious that she had halted the car outside the local pub. Nothing.

It would nag her for the rest of the day if she left it at that so she turned the car inwards, parked it, and used the car radio set to give Dun Laoghaire station an update before disembarking the vehicle again. As she approached the front door for a second time, she studied the upstairs window more closely. It was closed so it couldn't have been the breeze – light as it was – that caused the curtain on the left-hand side to move. But she was now more convinced than ever that it had moved, she trusted her sight. As well as pressing the bell, she knocked loudly on the front door this time and then stood back so that she could be seen clearly from any of the front windows in the house. After a few moments she tried the front door but it was locked. Then she moved along each of the ground floor windows but it was dark inside and she couldn't make much out in the dark interior.

Working her way around to the back of the house, she climbed over the waist-high wall and walked down the sloping small yard to the back door. Strewn about the yard amongst some overgrown bushes were old pieces of broken furniture, paintings, and a few large, cracked mirrors, their glass reflecting rays of light from the afternoon sun. There was no bell so she knocked heavily on the door, called out Balfe's name, tried the handle – which was locked – and stood back in order to be in clear sight. There were three upstairs windows and two on the ground floor, all looked locked and in need of a paint job and a good cleaning. She scrutinised them one at a time before pushing past a withered bush on the left of the door to get a closer look at the bottom ones. Using her right hand to wipe grime off a corner of the first one, she leaned in with her now dirty hand against her forehead to provide shadow from the sun and squinted to peek inside. Slowly rotating from right to left, she now noticed that the latch on the left-hand side opening was either broken or not fully pushed down and there was a gap of just under a centimetre. Just as at the front, everything inside appeared dark, still and dusty. Moving back from the window to check the next one, she suddenly froze. This time it wasn't her vision that picked up something, it was her hearing. A slow sigh or groan emanated from inside. The sound was faint and somewhat muffled but she was certain that it came from the interior and from a human being. Had Balfe fallen down the stairs and was in trouble, she asked herself? Or maybe he had suffered a heart attack from grief over his missing wife? Noreen called again, identifying herself as a Garda, and asking if someone needed her assistance. There was no response. She thought about reporting it to the station but she had just given them an update so her decision was to act.

Wedging her fingers through the slight opening, she pulled at the rusty, creaking metal window frame – about a metre in height and half a metre in width - until she considered it sufficiently ajar to climb in. Although she was slight in frame and in the guards' light summer wear, she quickly discovered that she had misjudged the size of the opening when she struggled to squash through it. Stepping back again, she used two hands to force the window further open but it was resisting strongly. Looking around the yard for a branch or long pole she couldn't find anything that would help with the task so she resigned to make one last effort before using her personal radio set – attached to the collar of her shirt – to request assistance. This time, she stood further to the side of the window and put an old cloth that she found lying under the window sill to protect her hands from the jagged edges of the frame's rust. Before continuing, Noreen stopped for a moment and held her breath to listen and look for any further signs of life inside. Nothing, so she gave the frame another sharp tug and it reluctantly conceded a few more centimetres.

    Clambering in as quickly and safely as she could, she found herself in what looked like a storeroom for smaller items as it had wooden shelving on two walls with a large number of clocks, vases and miniature statues kept there. All of the pieces were between thirty and forty centimetres in height and struck Noreen as having been left untouched and unloved for quite some time. The limited light coming in through the window made a few of the serpents and dragons painted on the objects caught in the glare look startled and dangerous, as if interrupted in the commissioning of a crime. Noreen had no desire to stay in this creepy atmosphere for longer than necessary. There was an open doorway on her right-hand side and she hurriedly walked through it.

The sight that awaited her stopped her in her tracks as if someone had cast a magic spell on her to freeze. It took all of her energy and willpower not to vomit on the spot. A man sat on a wooden chair with ropes encompassing most of his body, from his legs to his neck. Plastic tape covered his mouth and blood ran down his face from what seemed to be gaping wounds at the top of his head. The four legs of the chair were surrounded with blood. She assumed it was a man because she assumed Fran Balfe lived here but otherwise identifying the gender of this wretched individual would have been difficult, particularly as her eyesight was still adjusting to the blackness. The man's head turned towards her as she stood motionless and his bulging eyes stared at her. Noreen had never seen such fear before.

Nor did she see the silhouetted figure emerging from behind the door holding a double-sided hunting knife.

Chapter 38

St. Brigid's Ward on the third floor of St. Vincent's hospital on the south side of Dublin city centre had six beds for post-surgery female patients. All six were occupied when Hennessy arrived, awkwardly holding a bunch of orchids in his right hand. He was surprised when the text came through that his boss – although she wasn't his boss at the moment as he understood it – was allowed to have visitors. It wasn't exactly a summons to visit; it wasn't even an invitation in terms of its wording, but he took it to mean that he wouldn't be cursed out of it if he did make the effort.

Some of the woman in the ward struck Hennessy as being in very poor shape. There was an elderly couple visiting the woman in the first bed inside the door and, directly opposite, a well dressed middle-aged man holding the hand of a very frail-looking woman. The remaining four beds had their curtains pulled around them so he had to carefully check each one. Fortunately, the second one he peered in to – beside the sun-encased window – was the right one. But that wasn't clear to him on first inspection, he had to double-check. He hardly recognised Detective Superintendent Marie Brophy, not so much because she looked old and gaunt – which she did – but more because she looked vulnerable. As long as he had known her, she had a diminutive, spindly type of build but she was made of concrete. Her spirit and her feistiness set her apart from many of her peers.

Brophy appeared neither pleased nor displeased when she saw Hennessy, her expression remaining neutral. On the locker beside her lay a tray with bottles of cordial and a glass, and next to the tray a few magazines with two books on top. She was lying flat in the bed with a drip connected to her left arm. Hennessy held out the flowers and mumbled a greeting at the same time; there was no chair on this side of the bed so he had to stand, aware that he looked – and felt – clumsy.

'How did the operation go ma'am, you're looking good?' he lied.

Brophy's glare strongly suggested that she didn't feel the need to respond to such falsehoods, well-intentioned and all as they were.

'Good of you to visit detective; pray tell, how is the investigation going?'

Hennessy was taken aback by the direct question but then again, Brophy was never one for niceties.

'Quite well ma'am' he replied hesitantly. 'We have a few leads...people involved in the antiques trade, and who have access to the runway construction site...that sort of thing'

'So you've identified the victim?' probed Brophy.

'Well, more or less ma'am, we're pretty sure it's a Rebecca Balfe, an antiques dealer. She was reported missing by her husband, the description fits' answered Hennessy.

'Confirmed by DNA?'

'Not quite ma'am, we did get a sample but it wasn't clear enough. We're getting another one. And we're checking lists of people with access to where the remains were found so – '

'You need more detectives' interrupted Brophy.

'Yes ma'am, we do. I'm taking it up with the Chief Super – '

'Don't bother Garoid' interrupted Brophy again, showing more life as the conversation went on. 'Firstly he doesn't give a fuck if it's not gang-related, and secondly, there are no spare resources. If there were, I would have assigned them to you. Even the guy I did scrounge – who got stabbed – he was fresh out of investigating romance scams. I feel guilty now putting him onto a homicide team, he clearly wasn't ready'.

'Don't ma'am' said Hennessy in a more assertive tone than he normally mustered in discussions with Brophy. 'He's sharp and learns quickly; the stabbing had nothing to do with the inquiry, he just happened to be at the airport when the call came in. In fact, he did really well to spot that escaped deportee'.

'Be that as it may, you should have another ten staff on your team, at least. All of these new duties and taskforces - plus retirements of course - are leaving us severely depleted' said Brophy.

'Can I take it from your interest ma'am, that you're coming back to work?' asked Hennessy.

'Quite the contrary detective, the surgery didn't go well'.

Chapter 39

'You're not supposed to be ringing' snapped AJ when she answered.

'I've got two more names for you' answered an enthusiastic Lennon.

'Did you hear me?' snapped AJ again.

'I'm fine, honestly AJ, hundred percent, it was just a stitch or two that needed to be repaired. Nothing to do with work, I was back out in an hour' pleaded Lennon.

'If Hennessy found out that you were even thinking about – '

'It's grand AJ, I'll tell him I had this work done before the update meeting' interrupted Lennon.

'The update meeting that you didn't fucking update him about this work you had done before? He's a fucking detective Johnny!' said AJ sharply.

Lennon didn't respond.

'Okay, okay, give me the names' said AJ feeling a little guilty at her reaction when he was only trying to help.

'Right, the first is a guy you both met. Griffin, Mathew Griffin. Nothing connecting him to antiques as far as I can tell but he's showing up on Interpol's system as serving time for shooting someone during a robbery in Peru over a decade ago. Details are sketchy on what sentence he got or if the victim died but as you know, I'm forbidden from contacting Interpol directly to get more information. He's been getting into trouble since his teens, adopted, ran away from a few foster homes in Wexford, got in with bad company, that sort of thing. I'll email you the details. The second guy is Spanish, Romero, he – '

'Hold on' interrupted AJ, 'how does a guy who's been to prison for shooting someone in South America over ten years ago suddenly become a suspect in a murder case?'

'He has a criminal record AJ, and he had access to the construction site. Isn't that what I'm supposed to be checking? You expecting me to come up with someone who has a history of killing antique dealers?' This time it was Lennon who was doing the snapping.

'You're right Johnny, sorry' sighed AJ after a few moments.

'What's up AJ, haven't we agreed that we know who the victim is, Hennessy is asking for more people, and the three of us are trying to identify suspects; surely that's all good news?' asked Lennon.

AJ paused for a time, partly because she was contemplating how to put her thoughts to Lennon, and partly because of the noise from the aircraft taxiing past the conference room window on the nearby ramp.

'It should be....but I'm just not convinced'.

'Go on' said Lennon.

'Brophy would have given us more staff if she could have, the chances of anyone else in the Park giving a shit about this investigation are slim. Sorry to sound negative but that's how I see it' explained AJ. What she was really thinking but didn't want to say to Lennon was that she couldn't be sure Hennessy was the detective to lead the investigation. She say hesitancy that she didn't believe was conducive to a successful outcome. Then again, maybe her chequered history with Hennessy was clouding her judgement.

'Well then the three of us will have to plough on, that's all we can do. Focus more on enemies or competitors of Rebecca Balfe, as well as her husband of course' said Lennon.

'That's the other thing Johnny' said AJ.

'Go on'.

'Another potential victim has surfaced. An art criminal on Europol's watch list who flew in here with another guy recently, they're both missing but someone cut them up badly before that, nearly killed them. At least, we have a blood sample so we can check if it's her pretty quickly'. AJ deliberately didn't mention that these two might have been the two shapes she picked up on CCTV hauling the suitcase across the car park.

'For fuck's sake, I – '

'Shush' interrupted AJ, 'there's a call coming in from Hennessy, send me on what you have on those two guys, I'll give you the names of dodgy art dealers that we got from the antiques unit'.

'Gar, how did you get on with the Chief Super, ten more staff starting tomorrow?' joked AJ.

'You at the airport?' asked Hennessy in a serious tone.

'Yip'.

'The officer Dun Laoghaire sent to Balfe's for another DNA sample was critically injured, they're saying it's fifty-fifty' said Hennessy.

'What the – '

'When she didn't turn up for her shift change' continued Hennessy breathing heavily, 'they sent another car to look for her at Balfe's shop...stumbled on some sort of torture scene...two blokes legged it out the back...caught one...other one hijacked a car down the road...might be headed for the airport cos the one they nabbed had been looking up flights on his phone...they're not sure where to yet...I'm headed out to Dun Laoghaire now '.

'I'll alert the station here and the Airport Police, send me on a description of the guy and the car. What about Balfe?'

'Dead'.

Chapter 40

Texts and emails were coming in to AJ's phone as she made her way to Terminal 1 Departures. She was also communicating through her radio set. Cognisant that some passengers tended to get nervy when they saw Gardaí and Airport Police rushing around the place, they were trained to only run when in pursuit of a suspect or responding to a life threatening emergency. In full uniform and armed, she moved as quickly as she dared without attracting attention. Car park staff had been alerted to monitor entrance cameras for a silver Ford Ka, although the man they were looking for could be expected to have switched cars or even mode of transport by now, assuming he was heading for the airport in the first place.

AJ was thinking and typing on her phone as she roamed between the check-in islands on the

Departures floor trying to make her presence appear as a standard patrol. She had a black face mask covering as much of her face as she could. Passenger numbers were still very low due to the ongoing pandemic but there was still some twenty thousand people on outbound flights every day, about sixty percent of which used Terminal 1. The only description she had was a white, slim male about two metres in height with short, dark hair. There was nothing on his age range except that he was athletic in build. As she strolled around, several men came to her attention as coming close to fitting that outline but she ruled each one of them out as they approached the security screening process. One was part of a sporting group travelling to Faro for a tennis tournament, another was carrying a baby, and a third was pushing an elderly lady in a wheelchair. She was aware that the suspect could be using any of these approaches to avoid detection so she made sure to get close enough to make a judgement on their interactions with their travelling companions. The man she was searching for might have already passed through screening at this point of course or he might be using Terminal 2 or he may be hiding in some safe house. More information was needed on his description or his destination or both to have any hope of detaining him. AJ tried to ring Hennessy several times but he wasn't picking up, probably because he was interviewing the guy they arrested she figured. Lennon also had heard about the incident in Killiney and was trying to contact her. At least he knew enough to text her when she didn't answer. Staring down at her phone texting and emailing was a good way for her to give the impression that she was disinterested in the passengers walking about but a seasoned criminal would be unlikely to be fooled by it. From the communications that she heard on her radio set, all of her colleagues across the airport campus were doing their best but all were also struggling with the lack of detail.

There was also the question of whether this man was armed or not. AJ texted Hennessy and asked Station Control but she was none the wiser yet it made an enormous difference. Confronting an armed man in a busy public space was very different than confronting an unarmed one. She fully trusted the screening process to ensure that anyone who had gone through it was extremely unlikely to be carrying a dangerous weapon, gun or otherwise. Two other Gardaí on duty were trained to carry firearms with one directed to Terminal 2 and the other to the car parks. More armed units were on their way.

After about forty minutes, a call came across the radio that the officer in Terminal 2 had spotted someone dressed in a black suit who met the description, was travelling alone, and appeared nervous. AJ notified Control she was responding and made her way briskly out of the terminal and down the steep footpath towards Terminal 2.

It was his eyes that gave him away. Ten metres away, a tall, tanned man wearing a navy puffer jacket and a grey baseball cap fleetingly looked AJ in the eyes as he strode confidently up the footpath. It wasn't fear or panic in his eyes that caught AJ's attention; it was recognition. He didn't even break stride, continuing to walk with his hands in his pockets as if he hadn't a care in the world. Everything happened so quickly and yet weirdly in slow motion for AJ as she identified herself as an armed Garda whilst simultaneously drawing her Walther P99C semi-automatic pistol and pointing it, left hand under the right. The man's right hand – still in pocket - was already extending towards her and a bullet ricocheted loudly off the low concrete wall on her right. AJ discharged two shots in rapid succession and the man fell backwards. She sprinted the short distance, clamped her right foot on his shooting arm, and roared at him to remain still. Her whole body was shaking.

Blood was already oozing out from underneath his shoulders and meandering down the path, both hands still in their pockets.

Chapter 41

The sheets of paper around Johnny Lennon's laptop were growing larger, in contrast to his motivation levels. Every time he thought he was doing well, it rebounded on him. Being allowed to attend the meeting with Hennessy and AJ was definitely a step forward, even though he wasn't officially there. Then he starts bleeding again and it all goes to shit. Worse still, it was him that brought attention to it. Why didn't he hide it some way until the meeting was over, what the fuck did he think Hennessy's reaction would be?

When he went straight back to his research work – despite Hennessy's instructions not to – and found two people with criminal records, he couldn't wait to tell AJ. But then AJ pissed all over them. What was up with AJ anyhow, she's usually upbeat, and she's been so helpful to him since he joined the team? Was it something to do with her controversial past in the force that was getting her down, or more specifically something to do with her past and Hennessy? Now she wasn't taking his calls when he wanted to find out more about the incident in Balfe's antiques shop. For fuck's sake, even his former colleagues in the fraud office knew more about it than he did and he was supposed to be on the investigation team. AJ answered a few texts about it but with very brief replies. The real question he was trying to get at was if what happened helped or hindered the murder inquiry and he couldn't figure that out from her short responses. Maybe she's still trying to figure that out herself? The information that Balfe was sending him on people they did business with had dried up in any event, and it was only coming through in dribs and drabs when he was sending it. AJ did tell him that Hennessy was on his way out to Killiney so there should be more information later, not that he'd be first on the list to get it. Or maybe she's worried Hennessy will find out that she's communicating with him about the case when he's supposed to be doing nothing but getting better? If he didn't move about too much, he should be well healed up in a week he reckoned, ten days at the most.

Lennon leaned back in to the laptop and opened the file AJ had forwarded from the stolen art unit. Come to think of it, it was him that discovered the construction guy, O'Leary, was involved in that business, that's what led them to the art unit in the first place. The names were listed alphabetically and, where appropriate, the name and address of their business was included. There was a photograph beside each name, sometimes a formal one taken at a Garda station and sometimes taken by a surveillance team. One of the photographs was snapped at a wedding as the suspect was wearing a bride's outfit and the truncated arm of someone in a black blazer and white shirt was clearly visible on her shoulder. Under each name and photograph was a description of the suspect's background, family members, affiliates, and details of what crime or crimes they were investigated for carrying out and why. In some cases, a file was submitted to the Director of Public Prosecutions who had decided, invariably after a lengthy time period, that there was insufficient evidence to prosecute. Lennon knew from his own experience that when detectives went to the trouble of preparing a file for the DPP, they were almost certain of the suspect's guilt. It usually went down badly with the submitting officer, although not always a surprise, when the DPP didn't consider the evidence strong enough to secure a conviction. Occasionally, the name and rank of the investigating officer from the art unit was provided.

Slowly he scrolled through the names, carefully studying each one, and noting anything that might prove relevant to the inquiry. When he arrived at the third last name on the file, he stopped suddenly, leaned back in his chair, and reached for his phone.

Chapter 42

When Hennessy was called out of the interview room in Dun Laoghaire Garda Station to be told about the airport shooting, he noted numerous texts and missed calls as he hurriedly unlocked his phone. Details of the incident were still sketchy and he knew only too well that inaccurate or incomplete reports could spread like wildfire in such circumstances. The only people who knew the facts were the people directly involved.

His hand was shaking as he dialled AJ's number. Her phone was switched off. He looked at his missed calls and saw the last one was from Sergeant Tim Coady from the airport station.

'Tim, is she okay?' asked Hennessy with urgency.

'Badly shaken Gar but she wasn't hit' replied Coady.

'Thank fuck for that' sighed Hennessy.

'She wouldn't go to Beaumont so we got the doctor from the medical centre here to examine her. She's over there now. Chief Super is on his way and I suppose GSOC will turn up' explained Coady.

'What happened?' probed Hennessy.

'Gibson, from here, wrongly thought he spotted the guy in Terminal 2, AJ was responding from Terminal 1, looks like she walked straight into him'.

'And she downed him?'

'Like a stone, two shots. He got one off but missed' answered Coady.

'Dead?' asked Hennessy.

'Not when they put him in the ambulance I'm told, but not far off. Any word on the sergeant out there, McKenna?'

As Hennessy was answering, his phone showed an incoming call from Lennon.

'Nothing Tim, sorry, I've got to take this call'.

'Has AJ been shot?' shouted Lennon.

'No Johnny, she's okay'.

'What the hell is going on, two shootings in a few hours and nobody's telling me anything, I'm supposed to be on the fucking team, even if I'm on sick leave!' blasted Lennon.

'One shooting Johnny, knives were used in Killiney, and you're right, you should be kept informed' said Hennessy, as another incoming call was flashing on his phone, this time from the Chief Superintendent. He didn't take it.

'So, I was telling you at the update meeting that I'd asked Dun Laoghaire station to get another DNA sample for Rebecca Balfe. They sent a Sergeant McKenna, who seems to have stumbled on two guys torturing Balfe in his shop. When she didn't show up for her change of shift, they sent another car, two officers – who had an Uzi in the back of the car – were walking around Balfe's shop when the two gougers made a run for it out the back. They got one and the other hijacked a car. Balfe bled out in the ambulance and Sergeant McKenna may not make it. That's when things shift to the airport. With me so far?' asked Hennessy.

'Yeah, and AJ was at the airport' commented Lennon.

'Correct' confirmed Hennessy without asking Lennon how he knew that. 'I contacted AJ and briefed her that the guy on the run – which we had only a flimsy description of - might be heading for a flight. She alerted our people there and while they were waiting for more armed units, she came across the guy and shot him – '

'Wait' interrupted Lennon. This guy was armed but was using a knife to torture Balfe, and didn't use it when our officers arrived in Killiney?'

'Good points Johnny. It's all still very fresh, maybe he collected the gun somewhere after he fled Balfe's place or maybe they were just sadistic bastards that liked to torture people with knives' explained Hennessy.

'Was the guy they arrested armed?' continued Lennon.

'Not when they arrested him no, but maybe he ditched it somewhere in the house or when he was running off. As I say, it's early days' replied Hennessy.

'Go on' said Hennessy, trying to absorb it all.

'Okay, I've been interviewing this guy in Dun Laoghaire. He doesn't know we've got his buddy and he's blaming everything on him'.

'So he's talking, isn't that a bit unusual?' queried Lennon.

'He's trying to save his miserable skin, probably knows Balfe is dead even though we didn't confirm it, says he wants to do a deal and he'll tell us everything' said Hennessy.

'Do you believe him boss?' asked Lennon.

'I believe he's a lying scumbag who'd tell us anything to save himself and land his mate in the shit. He claims they dumped someone's body behind the airport car park but – '

'Jesus, he admits to murdering her?' interrupted Lennon.

'No, that's the thing Johnny. He says his partner was given instructions on where to find the body – in the boot of a car at the airport – and where to dump it. Claims the body was long dead when they put it in the stream' responded Hennessy.

'How does he explain torturing Balfe then?' probed Lennon.

'Same ol' shite. His partner drove them to Killiney and told him they had to find out from Balfe where some ancient Chinese vase was, one of a pair, says his partner used the knife on Balfe and McKenna, he couldn't stop him, yada, yada, yada'.

'So who was issuing the instructions?' asked Lennon.

'That's what he wants a deal for, claims he doesn't know their names but he'd show us where they met them'.

'They?' queried Lennon.

'Yep, says there was more than one. Thing is Johnny, a knife was used to torture two people in Santry recently and they nearly died as well' said Hennessy.

'Yeah, the art criminal that Europol was watching' said Lennon, immediately cursing himself and scrambling for an answer if Hennessy asked how he knew that.

Hennessy copped it but didn't pursue it.

'I was about to raise the Santry thing with him when I was called out to be told about the airport shooting' said Hennessy, when another call from the Chief Superintendent appeared on his phone.

'That's my boss Johnny, I have to take it. You know what I know now' said Hennessy.

'Sure, sure, thanks for that...hold on, hold on...I might know more!' said an excited Lennon.

'What?'

'I think I know who's giving the orders!

Chapter 43

Norman Prendergast closed his antiques shop early. His nerves were bad enough over the past few weeks but media reports about incidents at an antiques shop in Killiney and at Dublin airport had made them much worse. Sitting down at his desk, he again pondered how things had got to this point and, more importantly, how they would play out from now. He was under severe – possibly life ending – pressure to complete the deal, a deal he should never have agreed to in the first place. Easy to be wise about it now he told himself, when it's too late. He had tried every approach he could think of but none had worked. In fact, he had surprised himself at how patient he had been, particularly as it was costing him money, a commodity that seemed to feature strongly in every fuck-up in his life.

Eventually, he decided that there was only one option left: physical force. But of course that had required the deployment of resources that he utterly loathed being in the presence of or under an obligation to. Decision made, it should have been straightforward enough after that, just as it was with another task he had recently assigned them to. Straightforward for him that is, not for the poor unfortunates that felt the wrath of his representatives.

He could of course flee, an option that had been uppermost in his thoughts for months now. So much so that he had managed to place funds in an overseas account under an assumed name, should he opt to select that course of action. Even if he stayed put, these were funds that needed to be kept out of the grasp of the Irish tax authorities in any event. Staying put wasn't to be confused with 'fight' in that dreadful 'fight or flight' terminology as far as he was concerned. For Prendergast, not taking flight meant covering one's track as best one can and lying. This was a strategy that had served him well in the past, he reminded himself, so why change now? Well for one thing, he genuinely believed that his life was in danger now, from at least one source. Moreover, the guards were heavily involved now, putting his freedom at serious risk. But how much could they know, or find out for that matter? He had been meticulous in keeping his illegal activities at arms length, although it was impossible in his opinion to conduct such tasks without leaving some form of breadcrumbs. Technology had proved a double-edged sword in that regard; one could issue instructions using a device that could be easily destroyed but on the other hand, there seemed to be endless amounts of CCTV, tracking, duplicating and recognition tools out there also.

He was still contemplating his situation when the front door bell rang, followed promptly by a double-knock. Two men were standing outside when he opened it.

'Norman Prendergast?'

'Yes' confirmed Prendergast.

'I'm Detective Inspector Hennessy' said the man holding up a sheet of paper, 'you're under arrest on suspicion of murder, and this is a search warrant for your premises'.

Chapter 44

'Neither of you are on duty, understood?'

'Hundred percent Boss' answered Lennon, taking his seat in the airport station conference room.

AJ looked up from her seat and smiled.

'I just wanted to get the three of us together so that I could personally thank you. We got the DNA results this morning and the victim is definitely Rebecca Balfe. Also, the unidentified blood found on her glasses has been matched to Prendergast. He'll be charged with murder, along with his two goons. So well done Johnny for spotting his name as a business client of the Balfes and on the list of dodgy art dealers we got from the antiques unit'.

Lennon didn't respond, he was more interested in making sure his wound didn't reopen or if it did, that the thick dark jumper he was wearing kept it hidden.

'How is the sergeant in Dun Laoghaire doing Gar?' asked AJ.

'Out of critical care so she'll make it but won't be out of hospital for a while, lost a huge amount of blood' answered Hennessy.

'And the guy AJ shot?' probed Lennon.

'Still in critical care' answered Hennessy curtly, not wanting to dwell on the subject with AJ present. She had picked up her phone and started scrolling when the question was asked.

'Did Prendergast confess to killing Rebecca Balfe?' asked Lennon.

'I've spent the last few days grilling him and he vehemently denies killing her. We'll see if his tune changes when we put the blood match to him. If the bloke we caught in Killiney is talking any truth, it's something to do with a pair of Chinese vases, worth a few grand individually but ten times that when combined' explained Hennessy.

'So Rebecca Balfe had one of them?' probed Lennon.

'My guess is she either had one or both, or knew where one or both were. And maybe that's what led the murdering butchers to her husband, assuming it has something to do with the vases in the first place. We didn't find anything of interest in Prendergast's safe or hidden in his shop, and he had deleted all the CCTV footage from his shop's cameras. Nothing much in the Balfe's safe either: some cash, a few valuable coins and an expensive watch, but nothing worth killing for' answered Hennessy.

'What about the couple cut up in Santry that Hargraves told us about?' queried AJ, still looking at her phone. Lennon noted that something was nagging her.

'No sign of them and nothing to tie the two henchmen to, but it's definitely their style, brutality by knife' replied Hennessy.

'And the gun that the guy AJ shot was carrying, we can't match that to the bullet wound in Balfe's head?' asked Lennon.

'No, and that's the only gun we've found' responded Hennessy, wishing Lennon wouldn't keep bringing up the shooting. Hennessy knew that GSOC – the Garda Siochana Ombudsman Commission - was still conducting its investigation and he was also aware that AJ had been offered counselling by the force as it was standard practice in the case of a firearm discharge. Whether or not she availed of the offer he did not know.

'So this henchman we caught admitted to dumping Balfe in the stream but if that's true, how did she get from there to the construction site? Plus, he claims they had more than one boss so what were the different bosses getting them to do, did he ever admit to attacking the couple in Santry?' asked Lennon.

Before Hennessy could answer, AJ sat upright in her seat, held out her phone, and showed him a photo that Lennon had sent her.

'Is this what Prendergast looks like now?'

Hennessy took the phone and studied the photograph for a few seconds.

'Not exactly. His face is fuller and his hair is receding'.

'I need to make a call' said AJ, abruptly standing up and leaving the room.

Hennessy and Lennon looked at each other, equally confused. They could hear her talking outside the door but not what she was saying. She was still finishing the call when she came back in.

'Come on, we need to take a trip' instructed AJ.

'What? Where?' asked a startled Hennessy.

'I'll explain in the car, you drive Gar. You're coming too Johnny'.

The three officers got in to Hennessy's car outside the station and followed her directions, left at the airport roundabout towards Swords, left again on to the Naul road, and finally left in to the runway construction's fill dump. AJ filled her colleagues in as they drove.

The man they were looking for was standing beside a mucky digger when they arrived. He saw the car and slowly walked towards it. Hennessy got out of the car and lifted his jacket to show that he was armed.

'He ratted me out didn't he, the dirty bastard?' snarled Matt Griffin loudly, holding his arms out to indicate that he wasn't carrying a weapon.

AJ got out of the car and stood beside her door. She deliberately kept her jacket closed so that it wouldn't be obvious to Griffin that she was unarmed. Lennon had been told to stay in the car, mainly to request backup but also because Hennessy wanted to keep him out of harm's way. He knew that issuing the same instruction to AJ would have been pointless.

Hennessy didn't answer Griffin, he let AJ do the talking from a relatively safe position while he kept his right hand noticeably beside his holstered pistol.

'Identical twins have identical DNA' said AJ confidently, having just double-checked it on the phone with Lubenski. She let the statement sink in before continuing. 'Both adopted, both from Wexford, and both with photographs on our systems, but only you have a record of violence, and only you have access to the construction site'.

'You have fuck all evidence that I did anything. My brother is a useless, lying, coward, always has been, always will be' spat Griffin.

Hennessy drew his pistol and held it by his side

'Got sloppy when you killed that poor woman Matt, you left blood on her glasses. Would've shown up sooner but I'm guessing Peru didn't take samples when they charged you, or at least didn't upload them to Interpol's database. So, are we going to find the gun when we get search warrants, and maybe some stolen art?' said AJ.

Hennessy opened the back door of the car.

'Johnny, use my handcuffs, arrest him'.

Epilogue

The little boy was transfixed. Standing in the middle of a dark, dusty room filled with creepy statues and old clocks, he couldn't pull himself away from the stare of the dragon, its eyes beaming at him through the blackness.

'Theo, there you are!' said his mother grabbing him by the hand. 'All of this junk is being dumped by the builders, we can make it into a playroom for you and your sister if you like?'

When the mother pulled her son out of the room, the eighteenth century Chinese porcelain vase with a carved dragon remained standing on its shelf.

If you enjoyed this story, please post a short review on where ever you sourced it from.

Available now in the five-part
Airport Murder Mystery Series

***Book 1*: Forgotten**

A murdered girl is found in a suitcase on an airport conveyor belt. An armed robbery takes place in the cargo terminal the next day. The police officer who discovered the body, Anna Jenkinson, believes the two crimes are related but she's told to stay off the case.

She can't do that.

***Book 2*: These Roads He Walked**

Declan Cullen worked in the retail division of Dublin Airport. His colleagues and friends spoke highly of his support and good nature. When his body is found beside the airport boundary fence with the back of his head shot off, investigators begin to piece together the details of his life. Detective Anna Jenkinson is hand-picked to work on the investigation. This might be her last chance to make amends with her superiors for previous sins, unless of course she was chosen to fail.

Coming in 2024

Book 4 No Other Way to Die

There was nothing unusual about Darren Chandler's grey saloon car being parked on the second floor of the multi-story car park in front of Terminal 2 at Dublin Airport. There was nothing unusual about a family of four people heading off on a week-long ski holiday parking their red estate car beside her. There was something unusual about one of the family, Michael Finnegan, tripping as he got out of the car and feeling something wet and sticky on his right hand. There was something very unusual about Darren Chandler's bloodied body being found in the boot of his car.

Coming in late 2024

Book 5 Cancelled

Printed in Great Britain
by Amazon